Bello:
hidden talent rediscovered!

Bello is a digital only imprint of Pan Macmillan,
established to breathe new life into previously published,
classic books.

At Bello we believe in the timeless power of the imagination,
of good story, narrative and entertainment and we want to use
digital technology to ensure that many more readers
can enjoy these books into the future.

We publish in ebook and Print on Demand formats
to bring these wonderful books to new audiences.

About Bello:

www.panmacmillan.com/imprints/bello

About the author:

www.panmacmillan.com/author/francisdurbridge

By Francis Durbridge

The Desperate People
The Tyler Mystery
The Other Man
East of Algiers
A Time of Day
The Scarf
The World of Tim Frazer
Portrait of Alison
My Friend Charles
Tim Frazer Again
Another Woman's Shoes

Francis Durbridge

Francis Henry Durbridge was an English playwright and author born in Hull. In 1938, he created the character Paul Temple for the BBC radio serial *Send for Paul Temple*.

A crime novelist and detective, the gentlemanly Temple solved numerous crimes with the help of Steve Trent, a Fleet Street journalist who later became his wife. The character proved enormously popular and appeared in 16 radio serials and later spawned a 64-part big-budget television series (1969-71) and radio productions, as well as a number of comic strips, four feature films and various foreign radio productions.

Francis Durbridge also had a successful career as a writer for the stage and screen. His most successful play, *Suddenly at Home*, ran in London's West End for over a year.

Francis Durbridge

THE DESPERATE
PEOPLE

BELL

First published in 1966 by Hodder and Stoughton

This edition published 2012 by Bello
an imprint of Pan Macmillan, a division of Macmillan Publishers Limited
Pan Macmillan, 20 New Wharf Road, London N1 9RR
Basingstoke and Oxford
Associated companies throughout the world

www.panmacmillan.com/imprints/bello
www.curtisbrown.co.uk

ISBN 978-1-4472-1516-5 EPUB
ISBN 978-1-4472-1515-8 POD

Copyright © Francis Durbridge, 1966

The right of Francis Durbridge to be identified as the
author of this work has been asserted in accordance
with the Copyright, Designs and Patents Act 1988.

Visit **www.panmacmillan.com** to read more about all our books
and to buy them. You will also find features, author interviews and
news of any author events, and you can sign up for e-newsletters
so that you're always first to hear about our new releases.

Contents

Chapter One   1

Chapter Two   10

Chapter Three   21

Chapter Four   32

Chapter Five   44

Chapter Six   60

Chapter Seven   68

Chapter Eight   81

Chapter Nine   95

Chapter Ten   107

Chapter Eleven   121

Chapter Twelve   133

Chapter Thirteen   144

Chapter Fourteen   153

Chapter Fifteen   166

Chapter Sixteen   182

Chapter One

Detective-Inspector Hyde stood in front of an open window in the Royal Falcon Hotel at Maidenhead, and gazed at the river glinting in the September sun.

A tranquil scene, he reflected . . . and yet, in this attractively thatched, half-timbered old coaching inn, a young soldier had recently committed suicide . . .

Hyde's thoughts were disturbed by the sudden tearing of tyres on gravel as a silver-grey Lancia Flaminia drove into the courtyard and wrenched to a stop. A man of about thirty-five jumped out, and the constable on duty at the hotel's main entrance stepped forward.

"I'm Philip Holt, the dead man's brother," Hyde heard the young man explain tensely.

"Inspector Hyde's expecting you, sir. I'll take you right up."

As the two men disappeared from view Hyde glanced at his watch. Even with a car as powerful as the Lancia, Holt had certainly lost no time in getting from London to Maidenhead. It was scarcely an hour since the police had telephoned him in London.

A moment later there was a tap on the door and Philip Holt was shown in.

"You've made very good time, sir," Hyde commented as they shook hands.

"I got here as soon as I could, Inspector," Philip said. "I know the road. I was out this way only last night, as a matter of fact. I was one of the judges at a photographic competition in Marlow."

"You're a professional photographer, aren't you, sir? You have a studio in London, I believe?"

"That's right, Inspector. In Westminster, near the Houses of

Parliament. The studio adjoins my flat. But what on earth was my brother doing in these parts? I was astounded when I heard the news – he told me he was going to Dublin!"

Hyde raised his eyebrows at this interesting piece of information, but decided to defer comment for the moment. He observed the casually dressed figure with untidy chestnut hair and the serious features which, unknown to the Inspector, could so quickly be transformed into a smile.

"Do you think I could see my brother?" Philip asked.

Hyde nodded. "The body has been removed from the hotel room, but as a formality I shall have to ask you to identify him."

"Of course." Philip took out a cigarette case and lit a cigarette. His face was ashen, and his hands trembled slightly as he slipped his lighter back into his pocket.

"First of all," Hyde said quietly, "I think perhaps you ought to see your brother's room. Would you mind coming with me, sir?"

He led the way into the hotel corridor and up a flight of deeply carpeted stairs.

Room 27 was a hotel bedroom like many others, perhaps with a shade more comfort and decorative taste than might have been expected of a single room in an English hotel. The empty bed had been roped off, but there was no sign of detectives carrying out the customary minute search; evidently they had completed their work while Philip had been driving out from London.

There was a small bloodstain on the pillow, and a sheet of white paper lay on the night table near by.

Inspector Hyde picked it up. "It's addressed to you, sir." Philip appeared to hesitate.

"We've taken our prints, sir, it's all right to handle it." Philip took the note and read the simple handwritten message.

Dear Philip,
Please forgive me. This is the only way out.

Rex

He stood holding the note for what seemed a long time. Eventually he became aware of the mute question in the Inspector's eyes.

"Yes, it's Rex's handwriting all right."

"You're quite sure about that, sir? It's very important."

"Yes, I'm quite sure."

Hyde nodded and took the sheet of paper from him. "We naturally took photographs before removing the body for autopsy," he went on.

"May I see them?"

"Yes, of course. I suggest we go downstairs – there's a quiet room that the hotel have put at our disposal, where we can talk. As soon as the prints are ready they'll be brought to me there."

It was a private lounge to which the Inspector led Philip. The scent of fresh roses filled the tastefully furnished room, which was empty, and very quiet.

During their talk a plain-clothes detective tapped on the door and brought the expected prints, still limp and slightly damp, and the Inspector discreetly busied himself with his pipe while Philip studied them.

After a while Philip spoke. "You have no doubts about its being suicide, Inspector?"

As the Inspector slowly filled his pipe, relit it, and took obvious pains to choose his words, Philip studied him. Fifty-ish; thick hair going metal-grey. Rather on the diffident side – a mild-mannered man who had probably got where he was more through dogged persistence than brilliance or thrust. Not, however, a man to be underestimated; there was probably a good brain behind the quiet façade.

"Experience has taught me not to be in a hurry in such cases," Hyde said at length. "Nevertheless" – he indicated the batch of photographs with his pipe-stem – "from the position of the body, the angle of the army revolver – which has your brother's fingerprints on it and no other – and the suicide note which you tell me is unquestionably in his hand . . . from all this, the evidence points very strongly towards suicide."

Philip shook his head impatiently. "It doesn't add up, Inspector! Rex just wasn't the type."

Hyde coughed discreetly. "I very much doubt if there is 'a

type', Mr Holt. In my experience there's practically no end to the number of reasons why people take their own lives. One has to search into the deceased's background for some motive – strain, acute fear, or overwhelming worry . . ."

"Rex was never worried about anything in his life!" Philip exclaimed. "Nor scared. He was in the best of spirits when he left me on Monday afternoon. He'd just come on leave."

"The relationship between you was very close?"

"Very. We lost both our parents when we were quite young. I tell you, Rex was a happy-go-lucky chap, only interested in having a good time."

"Could he manage that, on a private's pay in the Army?"

"Well, it's all-found, you know. A soldier doesn't have to worry about rent or electricity bills or where his next meal's coming from."

"True, true. But how about when he was on leave?"

Philip's features relaxed for a moment. "I suppose you could say I was the fairy godmother there. As I said, there was no one else for him to turn to."

"Did you give your brother any money during this particular leave?"

Philip shrugged. "Just a few pounds – not much."

The Inspector coughed and played with his pipe, tactfully hoping not to have to ask the inevitable rider.

"Thirty pounds, to be precise," Philip volunteered. "In five-pound notes."

"Thank you." After a slight pause Hyde continued in his quiet tone, "The hotel management tell me your brother registered here at four o'clock on Monday afternoon. He booked the room by telephone the previous day, and arrived in a rented Morris Minor."

Philip shook his head with irritated bewilderment. "But why the devil didn't he tell me the truth? He told me he had to go to Dublin, that he was catching the three-fifteen from St Pancras. I put him into a taxi myself and heard him tell the driver to take him to the station. What made him change his mind and come to Maidenhead?"

Hyde looked a shade embarrassed. "I'm afraid he didn't change his mind, sir, it was already arranged."

"Yes, yes, of course, so you were saying – the room was booked and everything. In other words, he lied to me . . . All the same, it doesn't add up."

"Did he say why he had to go to Dublin?" the Inspector asked.

"Yes. A friend of his from his regiment had been killed in a street accident in Hamburg. Rex was stationed there in the B.A.O.R., you know."

"Yes, we got that much from his papers."

"Just before this soldier – a man called Sean Reynolds – died, he gave Rex a wallet and asked him to take it to his wife in Dublin. Rex couldn't have been lying! He even showed me the wallet! There was a photograph of Reynolds and his wife inside."

"Did you know most of your brother's army friends, sir?"

"Some of them. Not Reynolds, though, or his wife. She must be a musician, I imagine. In the photograph Rex showed me she was playing an accordion, with her husband standing behind her looking over her shoulder. Wait a moment!" Philip stopped in mid-flow and stared curiously at the Inspector. "Why are you letting me tell you all this, you must have found the photograph in Rex's belongings!"

There was an awkward silence.

"Well, didn't you find it, Inspector?"

"I'm afraid not, sir. There was your brother's wallet, with his pass, ticket, and so on; and the money you lent him, but there was no other wallet, and no photograph of any kind."

Philip looked blank. There was another awkward silence before the Inspector stood up, strolled to the window, and stared at the immaculate green lawn stretching down to the banks of the river. Eventually he turned and said, "Mr Holt, all suicides are puzzling, if only because the sole person who could tell us the facts is the dead man himself. But this case is more puzzling than most. The portrait you've drawn for me – and I don't for one moment doubt its accuracy – is of a light-hearted young man, in the best of health, under no financial strain, with no worries . . . Surely he wasn't the type to take his life on account of some unhappy love affair?"

Philip smiled. "I take it you've not seen the portrait of Rex in the showcase outside my studio? Typists go out of their way to stop and goggle at it. He was a fantastically handsome young devil. He'd only to crook his little finger and the girls came tumbling after. Women may have taken Rex seriously, but never vice versa." Hyde nodded and Philip went on, "That was one of the reasons why he liked army life; he used to say it gave him a wide field of action and the chance to keep moving so they couldn't pin him down. He wouldn't come into the photographic business with me – he said once you settled down to a steady job 'they'd got you'. Marriage, in other words."

"Are you married, Mr Holt?"

"I – I was."

The Inspector noticed the slight hesitation and tactfully waited for more.

Philip obliged him. "I married my secretary. After a couple of years the studio had a run of bad luck and I found I was in danger of losing my wife as well as my business. It cost me a packet to buy back my freedom. Rex said it should be a lesson to me."

"And now your studio is – er – doing well again?"

"If you mean the Lancia, that's mostly to impress the clients! I'm still up to my eyes in debt, but I'm just beginning to see daylight again."

"I see. Thank you for being so frank, Mr Holt. Now, to get back to your brother: had he any hobbies, any paramount interests in life?"

Philip paused before answering, stubbing out his cigarette.

"I think the old tag of 'Wine, Women, and Song' just about covers it."

"Would you care to enlarge on that?"

"Well, he wasn't a heavy drinker, but he liked his bottle – beer, rather than wine. His best friend was the most phenomenal drinker of beer I've ever encountered – a corporal called Andy Wilson . . . Women were certainly a major interest in Rex's life . . .

And as for song, he and Andy used to spend the best part of every leave sitting in a little music shop in Tottenham Court Road, listening to the Top Twenty or whatever they call it."

Unobtrusively, but with no attempt to hide what he was writing, the Inspector had taken out a worn notebook and was scribbling rapidly.

"Corporal Andy Wilson, you say? The same regiment?"

"Yes. He's on leave now, as a matter of fact. They both came off the Harwich boat together."

"And the music shop in Tottenham Court Road – do you happen to know its name?"

"Yes, it's called Pop's Corner. Run by a funny little chap named Luther Harris."

Hyde continued writing for a moment, then said, without looking up, "Pop records, women, beer – odd tastes to combine with a taste for poetry."

Philip looked faintly surprised. "Poetry?"

"Yes, sir. I understand your brother was fond of reading poetry."

"Whoever gave you that idea? Rex never read a word of verse in his life – at least, not since they gave up trying to cram it into his head at school."

Hyde was regarding him with quickened interest. "Are you quite sure, Mr Holt?"

"Absolutely certain."

"People are apt to be shy about that sort of thing, you know. Especially a soldier."

"Maybe. But Rex had no use for poets, I can assure you." Paradoxically, Hyde nodded, as though this confirmed some private theory of his own. He turned from the window and picked up a battered briefcase from the settee. Opening it with a key he produced a book and handed it to Philip without a word.

"*Sonnets and Verse,*" Philip read out loud. "By Hilaire Belloc. Don't try and tell me this belonged to Rex?"

"Have you ever seen it before, sir?"

"Never. Where did you get it?"

"Apparently your brother did nothing during the past few days except study this book."

"How do you know?" Philip said somewhat sharply. "Oh, of course, you've been making inquiries – guests in the hotel have seen him and so on?"

"Guests, the manager, waiters, Mrs Curtis – "

"Who's Mrs Curtis?"

"She's the owner." Inspector Hyde glanced at his watch. "As a matter of fact, I promised to have a talk with her round about now. She's a busy woman and naturally very upset by what has happened in her hotel, so I'm doing my best to fit in with her. Perhaps you'd excuse me, Mr Holt? I imagine I can get in touch with you at your studio?"

Philip nodded and rose to his feet. "You have my telephone number, Inspector. You should be able to contact me almost any time; if I'm not there, my secretary will take a message. I'll probably be kept pretty busy for a while with the funeral and other matters. There's the business of the Will, too."

"The Will?" Hyde inquired politely, his manner as mild as ever. "Your brother's Will, you mean?"

"Yes. He was due to inherit quite a tidy sum held in trust for him. It was due in a few months' time on his birthday."

"Oh dear, what sour tricks fate can play at times," the Inspector murmured. "Do you happen to know to whom the money will go now?"

There was a short, tense silence, broken only by the sound of a car backfiring. Then Philip said, "That's an awkward question, Inspector. It's an awkward answer, too. I'm afraid the money comes to me."

After the Inspector had made arrangements for Philip Holt to be driven to the mortuary he stood looking out of the window for several minutes, lost in thought. Eventually he was roused by a knock on the door.

"Come in! . . . Ah, Sergeant Thompson," he said as the door was opened. "Is Mrs Curtis waiting to see me?"

"Yes, sir. Shall I show her in?"

"Not just yet. Close the door and make a note of these items, will you?"

The Inspector's assistant made rapid notes as Hyde, his manner no longer quite so tranquil, strode up and down the room, listing various lines of investigation for his men to pursue.

"Have you got all that, Thompson?"

"Yes, sir.'

"Luther Harris and the music shop aren't urgent for the time being; just look the place over and report your opinion of it . . . I'd very much like to talk to Corporal Andy Wilson – the War Office or his regiment in Germany will have his address while on leave . . . Now, the story of the Reynolds accident in Hamburg is vital! Check on that, and also trace his widow and find out if she plays the accordion – again, the Army people should be able to help . . . Two last things: find out if there was a photographic competition in Marlow last night, and if Philip Holt took part in the judging."

Thompson looked up, his face alert. "Marlow? That's not really very far away from here, is it, sir?"

"I should like to know exactly how far, in terms of time taken to walk it, cycle it, drive it! And I'd like you to find out what you can about Holt's financial situation. It might be a little difficult, but you'll just have to plod away. He told me his business had gone through a sticky passage but was beginning to pick up now. I'd rather like to have some figures. And it might be illuminating to find out how much alimony he has to pay his ex-wife."

Thompson closed his notebook with a heavy sigh. "You sure you don't want me to find out how many teeth she's still got, sir?"

Inspector Hyde smiled briefly. "Now you can show Mrs Curtis in," he said.

Chapter Two

Inspector Hyde's deceptively gentle manner of interrogation was ideally suited to a nervous little woman like Mrs Curtis. He got the impression that if anyone had barked at her she would have burst into tears and bolted from the room.

She really was astonishingly small, Hyde reflected, no more than five feet two at the most. He judged her age as getting on for forty and, being a naturally tactful man, left it at that.

"I won't keep you long, Mrs Curtis," he began in his patient, reassuring manner. "This must be very upsetting to you, I do realize."

"It's a terrible thing to happen in a hotel, Inspector," she answered jerkily as she played with a brooch at the neck of her boush. "The bad publicity . . . and all these detectives and journalists wandering around the place . . . The staff are quite out of hand! And it's so upsetting to the other guests – I'm surprised most of them haven't left already."

In her youth she had probably been pretty in a fluffy kind of way, but the struggle to keep the hotel going after her husband's death two years earlier had evidently taken its toll, and the severe shock of a guest committing suicide was very nearly more than her nerves could stand.

"I assure you, Mrs Curtis, I appreciate your difficulties. I've instructed my assistants to be as unobstrusive as possible, and I'll do what I can to keep a curb on the newspapers. We'll be out of here just as soon as we have all the information necessary."

"But what is it you need to know?" Mrs Curtis wailed plaintively. "I've already told you all I can about the soldier. He wasn't a regular guest, we'd never seen him before, and . . . oh dear, it must sound a hard thing to say, but why on earth couldn't he have committed suicide somewhere else! A hotel isn't like a private house or a rented room, we have so many other – "

"Quite so," Hyde interrupted. Unless he was a trifle more firm they would be going round in circles all morning. "Now, I'd just like to confirm some of the points you told me earlier today. Mr Holt booked his room by telephone on Sunday, you said?"

"Yes. I don't know where from."

"I see. Did he say whether he'd been recommended to the Royal Falcon by anyone?"

"No. It was a very brief, business-like call."

"Did he have any visitors while he was here?"

"Not as far as I know."

"Did he appear to meet up with anyone already staying at the hotel?"

Mrs Curtis brushed a strand of hair from her eyes and glanced nervously out of the window. "It's hard to say . . . I don't think so. He kept very much to himself; he spent nearly, all his time reading. I never saw him talking to anyone except Dr Linderhof."

"Dr Linderhof?"

"Yes, one of the other guests. He's a German gentleman."

"Ah! A German gentleman . . . Tell me, Mrs Curtis: has Dr Linderhof stayed here previously?"

"No, we've never seen him before. He's been here a little over a week, I think."

"Have you any idea which part of Germany he comes from?"

"Oh dear!" Mrs Curtis made an effort to concentrate.

"Yes, I think so . . . When he signed the register he gave an address in . . . in Hamburg. Yes, that's it – Hamburg." Hyde stiffened slightly. "Are you sure?"

"Yes, Inspector."

He was silent for a moment. Mrs Curtis offered him a cigarette, which he politely declined, and she lit one herself and drew on it with short, nervous puffs, glancing from time to time at her watch.

Hyde decided to take the hint. "This will be tedious for you, I know, but I'd just like you to run over the events of last night and this morning once again, and then I won't bother you any more."

Mrs Curtis nodded and attempted a shaky smile.

No, she hadn't noticed exactly when the deceased had gone up to bed. There had been a noisy banquet in aid of the local Dramatic Society and they had all been tremendously busy. No, she hadn't heard a shot – there had been so many bangs and loud noises in the course of the gay evening, and when she had finally managed to retire in the small hours of the morning she had slept like a log. Yes, Albert the floor waiter was the first person to discover the body when he had taken breakfast up to Room 27 at half-past eight. And there were no guests in the rooms adjoining Room 27 – on one side was a bathroom and the room on the other side was vacant.

It was the same dead end as before, Hyde reflected. Everyone whom he had interviewed so far had told the same story.

"Would you say the walls are very thick, Mrs Curtis? I mean between the rooms."

"Yes, they are. The whole hotel is very old and solidly built. We have double doors on all rooms and special thick carpeting in the corridors. That's one of the main attractions of the hotel – the old-world atmosphere and the peace and quiet. Even when there's a noisy party down below the guests on the floors above aren't disturbed."

"An excellent thing, I must say," Hyde murmured politely. "In fact, you appear to have a very fine hotel here."

"Thank you. Of course, I'm very lucky in my manager."

"Ah yes, that's Mr Talbot, isn't it? I must agree, from the little I've seen of him so far, he struck me as being very efficient."

"Oh, he is," said Mrs Curtis simply.

"Now, to get back to Mr Holt during his short stay here: you say he received no visitors – did he receive any post?"

"Nothing except the parcel containing the book I told you about."

"Ah yes, the book of poetry which he devoted all his time to reading. Quite a recluse, in fact."

"He seemed to want to be left alone, so we respected his wishes."

"Quite so. Well, thank you, Mrs Curtis. I don't think I need to trouble you any more for the time being. I may perhaps want to have a chat later on, but I'll try not to be a nuisance."

Mrs Curtis gave him a shaky, relieved smile and rose abruptly to her feet.

As she reached the door she seemed to remember her professional manners. "Can I have anything sent in to you, Inspector? A drink, perhaps, or some coffee?"

"Coffee woud be very nice," Hyde replied courtesouly.

"Good. I'll have Albert bring it in straight away."

"Thank you. Would you mind if I kept Albert for a few moments? I'd just like a short chat with him."

"Certainly."

Albert wore the black-and-grey striped morning jacket of a professional hotel waiter, and a morose expression indicating that he considered himself the victim of an unjust fate. It was obviously with difficulty that he prevented himself from saying out loud, "I don't see why this thing had to happen to me."

There was no variation in the story he had already told the Inspector that morning. His quarters in the hotel were on the top floor, a good distance away from Room 27. He had heard no shot. He had no idea when Rex Holt had gone to bed. Yes, Mr Holt had appeared to be something of a recluse – "Didn't do nothing except keep his nose stuck in that book all day long."

Albert obviously relished the telling of his story, and Hyde listened again to his description of how he had found Rex Holt dead in his bed when he brought up the breakfast tray.

"Got the shock of me life, I did! And the old ticker's none too good, neither. The Doc told me I ought to be careful . . . and now this has to happen! Don't seem fair, somehow." Inspector Hyde suppressed a smile. "I mean, what the staff are saying, sir, it don't seem right for a thing like this to happen at the Royal Falcon. A fellow wants to blow his brains out, well he ought to do it in the park or in a cheap room somewhere, if you know what I mean? Not cause a lot of trouble and inconvenience to a high-class place like this! It's not fair to us, not fair to the guests. Not fair to Mr Talbot, neither, is it?"

"You all think a lot of Mr Talbot, I gather?"

"The best, sir! Strict, mind, but that's what's needed. He's done wonders for the hotel, he has. The Falcon's one of the best old coaching inns in England, and things was going right downhill after Mr Curtis died. Mrs C. was real shaken up, and it was just too much for her. Mr Talbot's knocked new life into the place, if you know what I mean?"

Hyde nodded and sipped his coffee. "I know what you mean. The coffee's excellent, too." He stood up and unobtrusively led Albert, now inclined to be garrulous, towards the door. "Thank you, you've been most helpful. I'm afraid I have a great many other people to talk to, however. . . ."

"The one you want to pop a few sharp questions to is that Dr Linderhof, if you don't mind my saying so. That's a rum bird if ever I set eyes on one! Be'aves like he's planning to blow up the bloody world!"

Albert, in his somewhat highly coloured fashion, had come uncannily close to describing Hyde's first reactions on meeting Linderhof. The German doctor was shown into the room by Sergeant Thompson. He did look rather like a schoolboy's conception of a scientist fiendishly planning to explode the universe. Piercing blue eyes glistened from beneath thick white eyebrows, the slight frame was stooped, and thinning silvery hair sprouted from his skull in unruly tufts. Dr Linderhof appeared extremely nervous – "A bad case of the jitters", as Albert might have said.

It was somewhat reassuring to learn that Linderhof was not a doctor of physics or nuclear fission but merely a good old-fashioned practitioner of medicine.

"May I ask what brought you to England, Doctor?" Hyde asked.

14

"I . . . I needed a rest, away from my practice," was the answer. His English was good, though the strong guttural accent was unmistakable.

"Oh? Working too hard, perhaps?"

"One could describe it so."

"Is this your first visit to England?"

"No, I was here before, once."

"At the Royal Falcon?"

"No, no. In London. But it was too noisy. A friend told me to come here if ever I needed absolute quiet."

"I see. And you practise medicine in Hamburg?"

"Yes."

"Had you ever met Rex Holt before?"

"No, never before."

"He was stationed with the Army in Hamburg, you know." Dr Linderhof shrugged. "Hamburg is a big city."

"Quite so. Tell me, Doctor, what topic of conversation did you find in common with Rex Holt?"

"Who said I had conversations with him?" Linderhof snapped.

"Several people have confirmed that fact, Doctor."

The German's face flushed with annoyance. "Idle tongues! People should mind their own business! I scarcely spoke to him, and I have never met him before, that is the truth. I came here to rest, not to talk!"

Hyde nodded pleasantly. "I'm sure that's true, Doctor. Nevertheless, you did exchange some words with him. What did you talk about?"

Linderhof shrugged his shoulders irritably. "How should I remember? Probably the weather or some such trifling thing. Oh, wait a moment . . . there was a book . . . yes, he had the poems of Hilaire Belloc."

"Go on."

"A little thing, no doubt . . . but I happened to notice what he was reading, and by chance I love poetry, too. I was thinking I had perhaps found a . . . a kind spirit, yes?"

"A kindred spirit?" Hyde ventured.

"Yes, that is it! A kindred spirit. But I was wrong, Inspector. Mr Holt was no genuine lover of poetry. No, no, I was much mistaken there."

"What makes you say that?"

Linderhof threw up his hands in an expressive gesture. "People who love poetry like to talk about it to one another, Inspector. I do not think Mr Holt even knew the name of the author he was pretending to read! And when I quoted some of the Belloc lines, ones which were in the book he was studying, he failed to recognise them. I assure you, Inspector, that young man was no genuine poetry lover."

"How very illuminating," murmured Inspector Hyde.

"The book has been sent off to the labs, sir," said Sergeant Thompson later that morning.

"Good! Let me have their report the moment it comes in, it's very important."

"Yes, sir. What did you make of the mad scientist, sir?"

"The who? . . . Oh, you mean Dr Linderhof?" Inspector Hyde chuckled. "On the surface he appears to be a perfectly harmless G.P. The only odd thing about him is that he seems to be scared to death of me."

"I noticed that, too, sir. Perhaps his mother was frightened by a policeman when she was—"

"How are you getting on with the count-down on Mrs Philip Holt's teeth, Sergeant?" Hyde cut in firmly. "The ex-Mrs Holt, I should say."

Thompson pulled a long face. "You haven't given me much time, sir. I've put a call through to the Yard and they've got a divorce case expert on the job. We might have some news by lunch-time."

"Good. And Philip Holt's finances?"

"I'm trying to trace his auditors now, sir, though heaven knows if they'll divulge any secrets. His bank manager closed up like a clam when I tried that angle. But I have got hold of one solid fact, via the local newspapers: there *was* an amateur photographic competition in Marlow last night and Philip Holt was one of the judges."

"Was he now?" Hyde said in a non-committal tone. "Good for Mr Holt, sir? Or bad?"

"It depends upon the way you look at it, Sergeant. On the one hand, it proves that he was telling the truth. On the other hand, it confirms the fact that he was in the vicinity on the night his brother died. I think what might prove to be illuminating now, Sergeant, if you've got nothing else to do" – the Inspector smiled as Thompson made a grimace – "would be to obtain a run-down, minute by minute if you can manage it, of Philip Holt's movements during his visit to Marlow last night."

Sergeant Thompson sighed heavily. "Very well, sir. And now shall I send in the Talbot-johnny?"

It was Hyde's turn to sigh heavily. "Thompson, you will remain a sergeant all your life if you don't learn a little tact. One does not 'send in the Talbot-johnny', one asks the manager if he can possibly spare us a few minutes of his valuable time . . ."

On first impressions Douglas Talbot was a typically, dyed-in-the-wool hotel manager. The cut of his suit, the freshness of his linen, the handsome, carefully shaven features, and commanding appearance were exactly what Hyde had expected. But something jarred. It took the Inspector a few moments to put his finger on it. Then he realised – the man lacked deference.

Most hotel managers whom Hyde had encountered in his private and professional life had presented to the world a modesty of manner and speech which, even if it were merely superficial, gave a guest a feeling of slight superiority. Talbot did not possess this subtle quality. Although what he said was perfectly civil there was a trace of arrogance in his manner which puzzled and intrigued the Inspector. Doubtless the man ran an extremely efficient and successful hotel, but Hyde could not help wondering whether such a manner might possibly rankle with some of his more sensitive guests.

The Inspector was not unduly surprised to learn that Talbot

had only devoted his labours to the hotel trade for a couple of years.

"Yes," Talbot was saying forcefully, "it had always struck me that the hotel industry in Britain needed gingering up a bit! Too much slipshod management, too many incompetent staff hanging about with their hands outstretched for tips, too many half-hearted amateurs dabbling in a business that's really quite simple if you tackle it with energy and the right methods."

"From what I've seen," Hyde murmured politely, "your methods seem to have been very successful."

Talbot smiled complacently. "Thank you. Of course, this suicide business is a bad blow, but it's amazing how quickly the public forgets."

Hyde nodded. "I'm so glad you can see it like that. I tried to persuade Mrs Curtis along those lines, but I fear she refuses to be comforted."

"Mrs Curtis is a silly lit—" Talbot began, then checked himself in time. "Her nerves are rather down, for the moment, I'm afraid. She hasn't really recovered from her husband's death, you know. He was killed in a plane crash a couple of years ago."

"And Mrs Curtis turned to you for help in running the hotel?"

"Yes. I was a friend and adviser of the family. It was a purely temporary arrangement at first. I was in the City then, on the Stock Exchange."

"And now you run the place almost single-handed?" said Hyde amiably.

Talbot shot him a sharp glance, undecided whether the words had a cutting edge. Hyde's pleasant smile seemed to reassure him. "Yes, now I run things," he said.

The Inspector nodded, and bent his mind to the task of extracting from Talbot every scrap of information that could possibly be relevant to Rex Holt's death. At the end of half an hour, during which the manager answered his questions with methodical accuracy and obvious intelligence, Hyde had learned nothing new.

It seemed that an utter stranger had walked into the Royal

Falcon Hotel, spent three days reading a book of poems, and then carefully blown his brains out. It was not very much to go on.

Over lunch, an excellent meal served to him by a pretty Irish waitress in the private lounge, Inspector Hyde mentally placed his cards on the table.

Suicide?

Or murder?

There was evidence on both sides of the scale, but there was still a vast territory of unknown facts to be sifted. For the moment he had little more than his intuition to fall back upon, and he was too cautious a man to place any reliance on hunches.

Philip Holt, the man who had known Rex Holt best of all, refused to believe it was suicide. Yet he had confirmed that the suicide note was genuine.

Rex Holt had been stationed with the Army in Hamburg, and Hamburg was Dr Linderhof's scene of operations. (Hyde smiled slightly at the unintentional pun.) Was this significant, or merely a strange coincidence? What was the reason for the German doctor's apparent nervousness? And the book of Belloc poetry that clashed so oddly with the dead man's character and tastes? Was it pure coincidence that Linderhof knew Belloc's work? As for the book itself . . . it would be interesting to see what the labs turned up on that.

Supposing it was murder – then who stood to gain?

So far, the finger of suspicion pointed solely to Philip Holt; but he was certainly the one who had drawn Hyde's attention to the awkward facts. Was this bluff again, because he knew that the Will would come to light sooner or later in any case? Or was it unadulterated honesty? Whichever way the scales were tipped, Philip Holt's alibi and his financial circumstances were certainly worth investigating.

Was there any truth in the tale about Sean Reynolds and the missing photograph? Either Philip Holt had been lying, or someone had stolen the photograph from Rex Holt's belongings. Or possibly Rex himself had destroyed it.

Hyde shook his head and mentally reprimanded himself for even attempting to guess at a solution so early in the case. It was his duty to keep an open mind until some further facts had been established.

Two of them were established by a telephone call that afternoon.

"Sergeant Thompson speaking, sir. I've got the dope on Philip Holt's divorce, sir. Seems he wasn't exaggerating when he said it cost him a pretty penny."

"How much, Sergeant?"

Sergeant Thompson told him.

"A year, do you mean?"

"No, sir, a month."

In spite of himself Inspector Hyde whistled.

"Made me whistle too, sir," Thompson rejoined. "Reckon I'll stay single!"

"What else have you been able to dig up?"

"I've got his movements at the Marlow contest last night. He arrived at eight-thirty, took part in the judging, and distributed some prizes. Never left the platform all evening. Time of departure for London: approximately ten minutes to midnight. That would bring him through Maidenhead just about the time the Dramatic Society's party was in full swing, wouldn't it, sir?"

"*If* he came through Maidenhead."

"Hardly any other way, is there, sir?"

"No. As you say, there's hardly any other way."

Chapter Three

Inspector Hyde sat in his office, contemplating the dossier on his desk. After a while, with an expression that was half frown and half smile, he picked up a pencil and idly wrote on the cover of the file: *Portrait of a Murder Suspect*. He gave it a moment's thought, then slowly added a large question-mark.

He was in a thoughtful, doodling mood; but, as the report was due to go straight up to his Chief as soon as it left his desk, he took an india-rubber and erased the pencilled comment before settling down to peruse the dossier for the umpteenth and final time.

Inspector Hyde, Sergeant Thompson, and a team of unobtrusive but highly skilled investigators had compiled an intimate portrait of Philip Holt; a detailed account of his affairs – financial, marital, professional, physical – comprising all the different colours to the pattern of logic and paradox which go to make a human-being in the round.

Under the heading "Affairs Financial", emerging through a welter of figures mysteriously and miraculously obtained, was the curious contradiction that a man of his undoubted talent should be unable to make a financial go of his successful business. The blunt and ugly fact remained that Holt needed money badly.

Under "Affairs Professional" was the puzzling fact that he had made his name in the world of photography as a portraitist, but seemed to enjoy dabbling in just about every other branch of the profession from fashion to calendar landscapes.

"Affairs Marital" included, among other items, his ex-wife's comments on this particular point.

"Mrs Turner, the former Mrs Philip Holt, who since her divorce has reassumed her first husband's name, quoted as one of the grounds for dispute Mr Holt's refusal to specialise."

That was not quite how the good lady had phrased it, Inspector Hyde recalled with a wry smile. The official dossier had to put it in more decorous terms, but what she had actually said, in between the third and fourth dry Martini, was, "The man's a bloody idiot! He could have swept Beaton or Karsh off the map if he'd bothered. All the big names were clamouring to have their portraits done by him – Duchesses were practically queueing up to get their names on his appointments book. All he had to do was be a tiny bit more polite, put himself out a bit, and he'd have had the most fashionable studio in Town. But oh no, that was asking too much of him! He said it interfered with his artistic freedom."

"Freedom to do what?" Hyde had asked diffidently, somewhat taken aback by the heat of her scathing tones.

"To photograph whatever took his wretched fancy!" she had flashed, and emptied her glass.

"What subjects did he choose, then?"

"Everything! People, insects, machines – anything his butterfly brain happened to settle on! Common murderers leaving the dock, evil old men loitering under the bridges of the Seine, caterpillars emerging from the chrysalis or whatever it is they emerge from. Everything and anything – the lot!"

"And that was where he began to lose money?"

"Precisely. You can't squeeze a very fat fee out of caterpillars and Clochards, can you? He completely ruined his chance of a career by refusing to specialise. And even when he did turn the odd penny, he either gave it to that no-good brother of his or else frittered it away on his silly cars."

"Cars? You mean he—"

"Yes. He never keeps a car for more than six months. He's like a little boy really – a little boy with a sixpence burning a hole in his pocket. He runs after new cars and ogles them like other men chase after girls. And, of course, every time he trades in his current four-wheeled passion for a new model he drops a cool hundred or two. No business head at all – an absolutely impossible man, Inspector! It would take a saint to live with him."

Hyde had probed further (while privately forming his own opinion of the not-very-saintly Mrs Turner), but had found little that added significant colour to the portrait of the man he was investigating. There seemed to be no "woman trouble". If there was a drink problem, the fault seemed more likely to have been on her side of the marriage than his. Other extravagances? Holt evidently spent well on clothes but, judging from some discreet inquiries made in and around Bond Street, not anywhere near the same stratospheric level as his wife. Hyde came to the conclusion that the chief grounds for the failure of Holt's marriage had been his inability to offer his wife the high standard of material luxury which she regarded as her right. Hyde had still not got over the distasteful shock of learning just how much alimony the good lady had demanded, and got.

The Inspector shook his head and sighed as he flipped over the pages of the dossier. It was all there – Origin, background; Modest but sound education; Meteoric professional career; Studio-cum-flat in Westminster; Clubs (R.A.C. and an obscure photographic fraternity); Outside interests (cars); Sports (swimming and squash at the R.A.C. and golf at Sunningdale). Did it add up to the portrait of a murder suspect? The shaky alibi and the urgent need of money (so neatly solved by the large sum left in Trust for the younger brother) – they were in the dossier too.

Hyde sat in deep thought, then closed the file, initialled a short note to his Chief, and settled back in his chair to fill his pipe. During his lengthy perusal of the facts he had gradually arrived at a decision. The Crown had no case for a murder charge.

Not yet. The Crown, however, might harbour its suspicions, and Hyde had no intention of letting these suspicions stagnate.

When the verdict came a few days later Inspector Hyde presented to the outer world a façade of unquestioning acceptance. To all intents and purposes he accepted the Coroner's verdict of "Suicide without sufficient evidence to show the state of mind of the deceased". Only those who knew Hyde better were able to guess what was really going on deep at the back of his brain.

However, one man who knew him well was prepared to hazard a guess. Sergeant Thompson watched the Inspector carefully as he examined the copy of *Sonnets and Verse* by Hilaire Belloc which had recently been returned from the labs.

"It got a clean bill of health, didn't it, sir?" Thompson ventured.

"H'm? Oh yes, the labs have cleared it as perfectly innocent," Hyde said, weighing the book thoughtfully in the palm of his hand. "I imagine they're right, as usual. Oddly enough, though, I can't quite swallow it."

"Why not, sir?"

"Well, a book doesn't necessarily have to have a hidden code or messages in invisible ink in order to make it . . . significant. You know, it might prove illuminating to toss this little book back into circulation. It might set a few things in motion again, things that have been stagnating while the book was in the hands of the Crown."

"Where do you propose to start, sir?"

Inspector Hyde reached for his hat and answered as mildly as ever. "Well, the correct thing to do would be to return all property to the dead man's brother, wouldn't you say, Sergeant?"

The Inspector stood outside the bright yellow door of Philip Holt's studio in Westminster and raised his finger to the bell. As he made to push it his eye was caught by a striking portrait of the late Rex Holt in a showcase mounted on the wall. "Typists cross the road to goggle at it," Philip Holt had said, and Hyde could now appreciate the truth in this remark.

It was not the first time he had seen this particular study; smaller versions of it had appeared in some of the Sunday papers. Rex Holt had indeed been "a fantastically handsome young devil", to quote his elder brother's words. Had he been too handsome for his own good, Hyde wondered? Was there just a trace of weakness about the jaw-line, a hint of overindulgence to the set of the full-lipped mouth? Was it, to be blunt, the face of a spoilt brat whose good looks and lack of character had drawn him into deep water? Or was he simply imagining things?

He frowned and pressed the bell.

The clatter of descending high heels sounded from within, and a moment later the street door was opened. A startlingly pretty face with green eyes smiled up at him.

"Inspector Hyde, isn't it? I saw you at the Inquest. I'm Ruth Sanders, Mr Holt's secretary. Won't you come on up?"

She led the way up a short, steep flight of stairs, and although the Inspector was a happily married man and very serious about his work he could not help admiring the sweepingly graceful line of leg and hip which preceded him.

She led him through an open office door, with a glimpse of a well-appointed photographic studio leading off at the rear of the room.

Philip Holt was not alone. At the large bay window, which commanded a fine view of Big Ben, the river, and part of the Houses of Parliament, stood a heavily built soldier. Hyde recognised the faintly simian stance of Andy Wilson, the Corporal who had been the dead man's best friend.

"I do hope I'm not intruding?" the Inspector said politely.

Philip Holt greeted Hyde from across a desk, as the soldier turned from the window. "Not at all, Inspector. This is Andy Wilson. You've met, I believe?"

Hyde and Corporal Wilson nodded to one another, and Ruth Sanders, watching with bright, intelligent eyes, detected a certain frostiness in the atmosphere.

The corporal made as if to leave. "Think I'll cut along, Philip," he mumbled, and shambled over to an Army-issue zipper bag.

"Please don't leave on my account," said Hyde hurriedly. "I shall only stay a moment. I really only dropped in to return this book to you, Mr Holt." He took the slim volume of poetry out of his battered briefcase and put it on the desk, among a pile of invoices, negatives, and photographic prints. "The laboratories have finished with it – it appears to be quite unremarkable – and you're entitled to have it back now that the case is officially closed."

"But *is* the case closed, Inspector?" Philip said abruptly. "The Coroner may have decided to call it suicide – he had to say something, and he couldn't keep us hanging about all day – but I'm not so sure. What do *you* really think was the cause of my brother's death?"

Hyde realised they were all watching him with sharp attention. From the pretty girl he sensed a wave of interest and sympathy; from Philip Holt a hot challenge; from Corporal Wilson – big, bumbling, ape-like Wilson, on whose scalp tiny tell-tale beads of sweat were forming beneath the thin, straw-coloured hair – from Corporal Wilson came the faint hint of fear.

It was not a moment for candour, Hyde decided. With his gaze resting coolly on Andy Wilson he addressed himself to Philip. "What do *you* think, Mr Holt?"

"You know damn well what my opinion is, Inspector! Rex didn't blow his brains out . . . some swine did it for him!"

"If you've got any evidence to substantiate that opinion, Mr Holt—"

"No, of course I haven't any evidence or I'd have come to you in the first place, Inspector ! But I'm still beating the same old drum: Rex just wasn't the type for suicide, and nothing will ever make me believe he wasn't murdered!"

Andy Wilson cleared his throat and swallowed hard, like an untrained actor summoning his faculties for his first speaking part. "What Philip means is, Inspector, Rex was a bit of a lad, a good-time Charlie. Chaps like that just don't commit suicide." His voice gathered authority as he warmed to his theme, and he ventured a grin at Ruth Sanders. "Bit of a fad with the girls, too, wasn't he, Ruthie! Never had any difficulty there, I—"

"For God's sake, Andy!" Philip reprimanded violently, and Andy's comment stumbled to a halt.

Again Hyde's gaze flickered over the trio, finally coming to rest on the photographer. It was obvious that Philip Holt was irritated. But why should he be irritated, Hyde reflected? Surely Wilson's coarseness alone was not sufficient to warrant the extreme expression of annoyance on Holt's face? The Inspector broke the silence by picking up his briefcase. "I'm afraid I must be getting along, Mr Holt." As he reached the open doorway of the office he turned, as though an idea had suddenly struck him. Fixing Andy Wilson with a penetrating stare he asked, "You're quite sure you've never come across Sean Reynolds in the Army? I know I've asked you that before, but . . ."

Andy Wilson looked relieved. "No, Inspector. Like I said, I reckon this Sean Reynolds chap's a myth."

Hyde nodded reflectively. "I'm afraid you may be right. All our inquiries have failed to turn up anything about him. There's been absolutely no backing for the story of a street accident in Hamburg, or an accordion-playing wife."

"Good God, man!" Philip exclaimed angrily. "I saw the photograph myself! Right here in this office! Do you think I invented the incident? Right here in this room Rex took out his wallet and showed me the picture of a woman playing an accordion and her husband grinning over her shoulder! Now why the hell should I invent that?"

Hyde shook his head stubbornly. "I'm sorry, sir, but we found no wallet and no photograph among your brother's belongings. And I'm afraid the Army authorities deny all knowledge of Sean Reynolds or the accident. We'll just have to leave it at that."

"You seem to be ready to drop the matter a damn sight quicker than you dropped your inquiries into my alibi, Inspector! Perhaps you think I nipped into the Royal Falcon on my way back from Marlow and murdered my brother? Don't forget the pile of cash I stand to inherit."

"Oh, really, Philip!" Ruth put in, visibly upset. "You shouldn't talk like that!"

There was nothing to be read from the inscrutable expression on the Inspector's face. "I'll be on my way now, sir," he said quietly. "Good morning, Miss Sanders, it's been a pleasure meeting you. Good morning, gentlemen."

Ruth accompanied the Inspector down the stairs to the street and Andy Wilson took a large handkerchief from his tunic to mop his glistening brow. "Whew! . . . I never did like the rozzers and that one's no exception."

"What's the matter, Andy, guilty conscience?" Philip remarked pleasantly as he went into the dark-room adjoining the studio to collect a set of prints.

"Call it that if you want to," Andy said loudly. "I just don't like people poking their noses into my private affairs, that's all."

Ruth overheard this remark as she came up the stairs. "Don't you think that goes for other people's private lives too, Andy?" she said tartly as she returned to her desk.

"Sorry, love, I didn't know you were so touchy!"

Ruth compressed her lips and pretended to immerse herself in a pile of work. As Philip came back into the room she added in a tone of restraint: "You'd better remember it next time, Andy. There wasn't very much between me and Rex; you know – and it was over a long, long time ago."

Andy was too obtuse to realise that the remark was not really aimed at him. He grinned at Philip, pawed Ruth's shoulders, and then shambled down the stairs, zip-bag in hand, muttering something about dying for a beer.

As it happened, he very nearly died between beers.

Two hours later the police found his body spread-eagled on the pavement of a street near the Elephant and Castle, midway between two pubs. Three bullets had been pumped into his huge beer-filled frame. Three bullets apparently fired from a fast-moving car. The eye-witnesses were honest enough to admit that they had concentrated more on diving for cover than in obtaining an accurate description of the car or the men inside it.

Inspector Hyde was the first to break the news to Philip and Ruth.

Ruth said softly, "He's not dead, is he?"

"No, Miss Sanders, but he's critically ill. He'll be on the danger list for quite some time."

"Oh, how dreadful! I feel ashamed of myself."

"It's not your fault, Ruth. You didn't shoot at him," Philip put in quietly.

"With my tongue I did. I was pretty sharp with him and I'm sorry now. It's just that – well, Andy always did rub me up the wrong way, even when he used to come here with Rex in the old days. I thought he was a bad influence on Rex and . . ."

"Mr Holt," the Inspector interrupted, "can you remember what time it was when Wilson left here?"

"Yes. It was only a few minutes after you yourself left."

"I see. And may I ask, have you both been in all afternoon?"

"I think so . . . No, wait a moment, I did go out for half an hour, just for a breath of air; that dark-room is an unhealthy place to spend too long in. I just walked along the road as far as Lambeth Bridge and back. Ruth nipped out to post some letters and deliver a batch of proofs over at the House of Commons." The Inspector raised his eyebrows and Philip explained. "Some of the M.P.s come here occasionally, when they want glamour portraits done."

"I see."

The Inspector took out his pipe and began to fill it. Philip waited for the barrage of questions which would pin him down to exact times – that had been the procedure with his alibi for the night Rex had been killed – but the questions did not come. Hyde seemed to have no particular interest in the matter, and his next remark came as a complete surprise.

"Mr Holt, you remember the book of poetry I returned to you this morning? Do you think I might take another glance at it?"

"Certainly." Philip began sifting through a pile of prints and correspondence on his desk, frowned, tried various drawers without success, then pleaded Ruth's assistance.

She gave him a friendly grin as she began a brisk search and added over her shoulder, to Hyde, "He's the world's most untidy boss. I swear he'll misplace his trousers one day and come to work without them."

"The flat isn't very far away, so I'd be all right," Philip muttered defensively as he continued the search.

"Ah yes, you live on the premises, don't you, sir?" Hyde said.

"Yes, the flat adjoins the studio. There's a connecting passage through there." He indicated one of the doors leading from the office. "It's very convenient."

Ruth stopped searching and stood back. "I just don't get it," she said frowning. "It can't have vanished into thin air! I remember seeing the Inspector put it on the corner of the desk here . . ."

Hyde let them hunt a little longer, then, satisfied, he said quietly, "I don't think you'll find the book, Mr Holt. As a matter of fact, I have it here with me." He opened his briefcase and extracted the book.

Philip and Ruth looked stupefied."

"How on earth did it get into your hands again?"

"It was in the zip-bag Corporal Wilson was carrying."

"In the zip-bag . . . ? You mean Andy took the book from my desk?"

"He must have done, sir, unless you gave it to him."

"Of course I didn't give it to him! Why on earth should I do that?"

"I don't know why, sir," Hyde said steadily. "Now, I'd like you to think carefully. Was there any moment when he could have slipped it out of sight without your noticing?"

"No . . . I don't think so. We were with him all the time."

"Miss Sanders wasn't here all the time, sir. She very kindly escorted me down the stairs to the street. Where were you at that moment?"

"Good Lord! It's true, I went into the dark-room for a few seconds. Well I'll be damned! I always did say Andy was a rogue, but I didn't think—"

The rest of his sentence was cut off by the ringing of the telephone.

Ruth answered it, then turned to Hyde. "It's for you, Inspector."

"Oh. I do hope you don't mind," the Inspector apologised. "I left word that I could be reached here if there was anything important."

Philip nodded his understanding and Ruth handed Hyde the phone.

"Hyde speaking . . . Yes . . . Yes, go on, Sergeant . . . When was this? . . . I see . . . Is he still delirious? . . . Right! . . . No, don't do that, stay right with him, I'll keep in touch. Thank you for ringing."

He replaced the receiver thoughtfully. "That was from the Middlesex Hospital. Andy Wilson is talking. He's delirious, but some of it makes sense – or nonsense, I'm not sure which."

"What is he saying?"

"Apparently he's speaking of you, sir. He says: 'Philip – destroy the photograph.' "

There was a silence, broken by Ruth who slowly repeated the phrase. " 'Destroy the photograph . . .'? What photograph? We've got thousands of photographs in the studio. Which one is he talking about?"

Inspector Hyde said nothing; he continued to gaze at Philip.

The gleam of an idea flickered in Philip's eyes. "It would be odd if he meant the one of Reynolds and his wife, wouldn't it, Inspector?"

"It would indeed," the Inspector agreed.

"Then perhaps you'd believe that such a picture really exists . . . or did exist?"

Hyde made no comment.

" 'Destroy the photograph,' " Philip mused. "That's all very well, Andy old chap, but how the devil can I when I haven't got it?"

He began to pace up and down the room, while Hyde regarded him with undisguised interest.

"I'll tell you what, though: I'd give a lot to be able to lay my hands on that photograph again."

Less than twenty-four hours later he had good cause to remember those words.

Chapter Four

The telephone on Inspector Hyde's desk rang the following morning and Philip Holt's excited voice sounded on the end of the line.

"I've some news for you, Inspector! I've got something to tell
you!"

"Go ahead – I'm listening . . ."

"My secretary was late this morning, so I opened the post
myself. There was a large envelope, with nothing on the outside
except my address and a London postmark. I've kept it for you to
examine."

"Good. Go on, sir."

"Inside the envelope there was a photograph. It was my brother's portrait – an exact copy of the study in the showcase outside
my studio!"

"One which you yourself had taken?"

"Precisely, Inspector! Well, when Miss Sanders came in we spent
some time trying to puzzle the matter out, and eventually we decided
it must be a practical joke – that someone had, in fact, taken the
portrait out of the showcase and sent it through the post."

"A joke in remarkably poor taste, I should say," commented
Hyde. "*Was* it the portrait from the showcase, Mr Holt?"

"That's the extraordinary thing, Inspector – Rex's portrait had
gone from the case, but in its place was the picture of Sean Reynolds and his wife with the accordion!"

There was a long, tense silence while Hyde evidently took this
in, then he said, "How very odd . . ."

"I'm hoping you'll be able to find out who the couple are,"
Philip said eagerly. "Then maybe we shall get somewhere at last."

"I'll certainly look into the matter, sir. I'll send someone round right away to pick up the photographs and the envelope, and examine the showcase."

"Fine! I'm going to be out this morning, but Miss Sanders will be here."

"What exactly are your plans, if I might ask?"

Philip was slightly taken aback by the question. "As a matter of fact, Inspector, I'm planning to take a day off from the studio and play the sleuth myself, if you've no objections. I can be reached at the Royal Falcon Hotel, Maidenhead, and I hope to spend my time out there studying the guests' register. Is that permissible?"

Ruth could scarcely contain her excitement: but there was a tinge of irony in Hyde's voice as he replied, "It's a free country, sir."

Philip was about to ring off when the Inspector added: "Oh, just one more question, Mr Holt. Can you or Miss Sanders recall when you last noticed the showcase – before it had been disturbed, that is?"

"Oh – I'm not sure . . . You know how it is – you see the same thing day after day, and you hardly notice . . ."

"Quite so. Tell me: who's idea was it? To look in the showcase, I mean. Was it yours, or Miss Sanders'?"

Philip paused to think for a moment. "I'm damned if I can remember. It was Ruth's idea, I believe."

It was perhaps fortunate for Philip Holt that Talbot, the manager of the Royal Falcon Hotel, was out when he called, otherwise his request to be allowed to search through the register might well have been refused. Mrs Curtis dithered about in her perpetually distracted manner, but her reluctance was eventually overcome.

"What I very badly want, Mrs Curtis," said Philip, turning on all the considerable charm at his disposal, "are the names and addresses of all the guests staying at the hotel during the week leading up to my brother's death."

"Oh dear. . . . that's rather unusual, isn't it? I mean . . . I suppose it's all right, but really, I can't quite see why you want to look at . . ."

"Because I'm not at all happy about the Coroner's verdict, Mrs Curtis. I flatly refuse to believe that my brother committed suicide! I intend to dig further; the police are asleep on their feet!"

"Oh dear . . . I thought Inspector Hyde such a very delightful man – a real gentleman . . ."

"That's just my point – he's *too* gentle. I wish he'd been more active! He's wasted precious time – mostly making inquiries about me – and I'd like to see him taking an interest in the real criminals in this case. For instance, those thugs who shot at Andy Wilson in broad daylight yesterday!"

"Shot at Andy Wilson?" Mrs Curtis fluttered distraught eyelids at him. "I'm afraid I don't quite follow you."

"Didn't you read about it in the papers, Mrs Curtis?"

She shook her head and gave him a smile that in her youth would doubtless have been provocative, but was now merely coy.

Philip gave an account of the shooting of Andy Wilson and ended by saying, "It's my opinion that the attempt to kill Wilson was connected with my brother's death."

"Oh. Oh dear, how dreadful! Do the police think so too?"

"I really don't know what the police think. And I'm tired of sitting around waiting for them to get cracking! That's why I want to do a little investigating on my own account." He smiled at her, hoping to win her approval.

He apparently won it – or at least, she gave her consent to his request to see the register. "Yes, all right, Mr Holt, but I must tell you, all the guests staying here at the time of . . . at the time, were personally well known to me. Except Dr Linderhof, of course."

"Ah yes, the doctor from Hamburg. I wonder if there's any chance of my having a chat with him?"

Mrs Curtis uttered a tinkling laugh of despair. "Just imagine! Dr Linderhof left this morning after breakfast."

"Damnation!"

Philip looked as though he would have liked to enlarge on this mild oath, but he was not sure that Mrs Curtis's frail nerves would stand it. He hastily resumed his pleasantest expression, and she fluttered her eyelashes at him and went to fetch the guests' register.

She then escorted him to a private lounge where she promised he could work undisturbed, but to Philip's disappointment she remained in the room while he made a note of all the names and addresses entered during the relevant period. He asked as many questions concerning the guests as he dared and was nearing the end of his list when Albert, the morose waiter who had given evidence at the Inquest, came in with a message and Mrs Curtis was called away.

Philip seized the opportunity and slipped a Japanese pocket camera from his briefcase. Rapidly he took photographs of the pages which he thought might prove interesting; he had hoped to do this in the first place, but had feared that Mrs Curtis might disapprove and withdraw her consent. By the time she came back the register was recorded on microfilm and the tiny camera out of sight.

He was finally putting away his notes and thanking Mrs Curtis for her co-operation when a further diversion occurred.

The door to the lounge was partly opened, without any preliminary knock, and one half of a tall, thin body draped itself round the door jamb.

"Oh, sorry, Vanessa, I didn't know you had a gentleman caller," came an affected nasal drawl.

"Come in, Thomas." Mrs Curtis seemed rather flustered. "Come and meet Mr Philip Holt."

The rest of the sinuous body untwined itself from the doorway and appeared in full view.

Mrs Curtis gave an uneasy little laugh. "Mr Holt, may I introduce my brother – Thomas Quayle."

Thomas Quayle was quite a sight. Several inches taller than his sister, his extraordinary thinness made it seem even more. He was dressed in a dark blue suit with excessively high lapels and trousers of the narrowest cut. The whole startling effect was crowned by a white carnation in his buttonhole and an unlit cigarette in a white holder. In his arms he carried a small white dog.

Philip held out his hand, and the hand extended in response was so limp-wristed that he wondered why it didn't drop off.

"This is indeed a pleasure. Philip Holt, did you say, Vanessa? *The* Philip Holt? Didn't I see a *splendid* exhibition of your work in Fleet Street some while ago?"

"That *was* rather a long time ago," Philip answered, pleased despite the obvious flattery.

"It definitely lodged in my mind, though. I remember the Clochards in particular, with the misty Seine in the background. And your Shakespeare Survey. Not the sort of photography one quickly forgets."

"Thank you."

"Beastly business about your brother, I must say. You have my deepest condolences. So upsetting, that sort of thing. It must have been a frightful shock for you."

"Yes, it was."

"I understand you were under the impression that he was in Ireland at the time?"

"Yes, he told me he was going to Dublin."

Quayle stroked the smooth white coat of the tiny dog in his arms and added musingly, "What an extraordinary thing."

Mrs Curtis looked uncomfortable. "Thomas, if you don't mind . . ."

"That's quite all right," Philip said quickly. "I've more or less finished. I'll be on my way."

Quayle opened the door with a sweeping gesture and stood to one side as Philip gathered up the last of his notes and stuffed them into his briefcase.

"I do hope you've got another exhibition coming along soon, Mr Holt?" Quayle asked.

"I'm afraid not. The advertising agencies are keeping me pretty busy. It's not Art with a capital A but I need the cash."

Quayle sighed. "Ah yes, the sordid pecuniary facts of life. How I sympathise!"

"Are you in the hotel business, may I ask?" said Philip, suddenly curious.

Quayle raised one limp hand in mock horror. "Heaven forbid! Greasy dishes and hot-water bottles for the old fogeys? Not for me. I leave that department to Vanessa here. No, I'm in antiques. I've a little place down in Brighton. It's not exactly Mallett's, but it helps to keep me out of mischief. Doesn't it, Whitie?" he added, fondling the little dog's head.

"Thomas, for heaven's sake . . ." Vanessa Curtis protested.

Philip hastily cut in with his farewells and left the room.

As he was about to leave the hotel Albert called out from behind the bar, where he appeared to be cleaning, and indicated that he would like a word in private. Philip nodded and was waiting near the front entrance for Albert to join him when his eye alighted on a lilac-coloured Austin parked on the forecourt. Thomas Quayle's, he wondered? It seemed to fit his personality. As he crossed to look more closely at the car Albert came hurrying over, slightly out of breath.

He produced a Yale key. "I think this belonged to your brother, sir.'"

"Oh, thank you."

"Doreen, the maid, found it in his room. Number 27."

"It must be the key to my flat. I lent it to Rex on his last leave. I'm surprised the police didn't find it when they searched the room."

"It fell down a crack between the floorboards, sir. Doreen wouldn't never have come across it if they hadn't decided to redecorate the room after your . . ." Albert trailed off into an embarrassed silence.

"I quite understand," Philip said quietly.

Albert continued to hover expectantly, cleaning a scarcely perceptible smudge from the bonnet of the lilac car.

Philip produced the tip the man was so obviously hoping for. "Is that Mr Quayle's car?" he asked pleasantly.

"Oh, thank you, sir! No, sir – I don't know where his is." He looked round vaguely. "This one belongs to Mrs Curtis."

"Oh, I see." Philip thanked Albert and climbed into his Lancia.

He drove back to Westminster. Normally the other cars on the road would have excited his approval or criticism, but, deep in thought, he scarcely noticed them. His mind was on the pile of notes he had made during his interview with Vanessa Curtis. He felt he had achieved very little and experienced a strong feeling of frustration at being unable to talk to Dr Linderhof.

After garaging the Lancia he walked round to his front door and slipped the key which Albert had given him into the lock. It refused to turn; something in the mechanism seemed to have jammed. He had just removed the key from the lock to examine it when the door was opened.

"I saw you from the window," said Ruth. "You've got a visitor."

"Is it anyone important? I've got rather a lot to do and—"

"I think you'll find time for this caller," she said as they climbed the stairs. "It's that German doctor who was at the hotel – Dr Linderhof."

"My God!" Philip looked startled. "Yes, yes, I'll see him, Ruth! Did he say what he wanted?"

She shook her head. "He wouldn't tell me. He seemed a bit upset."

Dr Linderhof was pacing nervously up and down the office, peering short-sightedly at the many portraits, nature studies, and landscapes which hung in modern rimless frames on the walls. When Philip came into the room the doctor's face was a baffling mixture of relief and apprehension. It was a look a dentist gets to know well: the patient bracing himself for the ordeal, knowing he will feel better when it is all over.

"Hello, Doctor. I thought you'd left for Germany."

"My flight leaves this afternoon. I just have time to call on you before I leave."

"I'm very glad to see you. What's on your mind?"

Linderhof glanced apprehensively at Ruth, who tactfully withdrew from the office.

The doctor waited until the door was closed. "I have something which I must tell," he said in a low voice. "I cannot go back to Germany with a quiet mind until I say it to someone. It is about your brother."

Philip tried to prevent his voice from betraying a surge of excitement. "Won't you sit down?"

Linderhof shook his head impatiently, and drew a deep breath. "It is not my opinion that your brother shot himself."

"It's not mine either, Doctor. Have you anything concrete to go on?"

Linderhof shook his silver hair. "I do not know what really happened that night, but I am certain it was not self-killing. I tell you . . . I do not feel well from time to time, I have an ulcer and sometimes it makes me trouble, especially during the night. That night I had to get up and go along the corridor to the bathroom. I was wearing bedroom shoes and the carpets at the hotel are very thick, so that is why no one heard me. Do you remember where the bathroom is, the one on the second floor at the Royal Falcon, Mr Holt?"

"Yes. Next door to Room 27."

"Correct. Next to the room where your brother was sleeping. But he was not sleeping; he was quarrelling. I heard angry voices."

"You're sure the voices came from Room 27 and not from any other room?"

"Yes. There is no room on the other side of the bathroom. The angry voices were coming from Number 27!"

"Did you hear what was said, Doctor? Have you any idea what the quarrel was about?"

"Not everything. Only a little. But when they were shouting I heard your brother say, 'I am going back to London, I am not waiting another minute hanging around here with that damn book!' That is what he said."

"You're sure of that? You're certain that's what he said?"

"Oh yes. I heard that quite plain."

"And the man he was quarrelling with – what did he say?"

"It was not a man, Mr Holt." Linderhof hesitated, his ice-blue eyes gleaming with disturbing brilliance. "It was a woman's voice."

"Could you hear what she was saying?"

"She said, 'If I were you I would wait, even if you stay here the rest of the week.' And your brother is shouting then, very angry, 'I am not waiting a day longer and that is final!'"

"What happened then?"

"She must have begged him to lower his voice. I did not hear any more. I did not want to. It is not nice to . . . to listen – to overhear. I went back to my room. In the morning I learned with a terrible fright that your brother was dead, shot in the head."

"And you didn't hear the shot?"

"Oh no. Such a thing I would, of course, have told to the police."

Philip paced the room, trying to make up his mind how much truth there was in what the wild-looking man had told him. Eventually he said: "What puzzles me is why you *didn't* go to the police with your information. I presume you didn't tell them, or it would have come out at the Inquest?"

"No, I did not tell them," Linderhof muttered uneasily.

"Why didn't you tell them, Doctor? Was it simply because you couldn't identify the woman?"

Linderhof's reply rooted Philip to the floor. "I could identify her. It was Mrs Curtis."

"Mrs Curtis? The owner of the hotel?"

"Yes."

"You are absolutely certain?"

"Positive. She has a voice . . . a little voice, like a complaining child; it is quite unmistakable."

Philip gazed keenly at the doctor. He was growing steadily convinced that the man was telling the truth. And yet . . .?

"It beats me, Dr Linderhof! Here you are, in possession of a vital piece of evidence, and yet you come to me instead of to the police. Why? What on earth prevented you from telling all this to Inspector Hyde?"

The little German seemed to screw himself into a knot of embarrassment. He shrugged his shoulders and muttered something incomprehensible in his native tongue.

"All right, Doctor, this is just between the two of us. I give you my word it will go no further."

"That is good; it must be, as you say, between the two of us. I cannot talk to the police because . . . because I do not wish publicity of any kind at this moment. I am ruined by one hint of scandal. Next week I must stand before a Medical Tribunal in Hamburg. There are . . . certain charges against me. If things go badly for me I shall not ever be allowed to practise medicine again."

"What are the charges?"

"Lies!" Linderhof stammered, his face flushed with anger. "Only lies, made up by idle people with nothing better to do than push their noses into other people's business! It is boring for you, the details, Mr Holt, but I shall clear my good name, you can be certain. That is why I came to England, so that no German newspapers can find me, and that is why I cannot permit myself to be mixed up in any matter with your police. My position is very difficult."

"I see . . ."

It was a strange story, but it had a ring of truth. It must have caused the little man a severe struggle with his conscience before he decided to go even as far as this.

"It's very good of you to come to me, Doctor. I appreciate it."

"You do? Then you will do me a small favour in return?"

"Certainly, if I can."

"If you make use of this piece of information, please do not mention my name during the next few days. After next week, when my trial is over, it will not matter one way or the other."

"Very well, Doctor."

"Thank you. *Auf Wiedersehen,* and good luck to you."

"Thank you. And good luck to you too, Doctor."

They shook hands, and Philip led the way down the stairs to the street.

When he came up again Ruth was standing in the middle of the office, her eyes sparkling with excitement.

"You've been listening," said Philip quietly.

She grinned mischievously. "It's all part of an efficient secretary's duties to know what her boss is doing during office hours, you know."

Philip was feeling tense and in no mood for Ruth's frivolous chatter. He was on the point of a sharp retort when the telephone rang.

"Saved by the bell!" she quipped, and he could not suppress a frown of annoyance. As she lifted the receiver she became the efficient secretary. "Holt Photographs . . . Yes, who is it speaking? . . . Just a moment please. – It's Mrs Curtis. She wants to talk to you."

Philip took the receiver. "Hello, Mrs Curtis? Philip Holt here. What can I do for you?"

Ruth watched him carefully as he listened.

He frowned slightly and felt in his pocket. "Yes . . . Yes, I still have the key . . . You may well be right, it certainly didn't seem to fit my door. . . . All right, Mrs Curtis, I'll let you have it back . . . No, no, I'd much rather bring it to you personally if it's important . . . No, it's no trouble at all . . . I'll call at the hotel tomorrow . . . Yes, Mrs Curtis, that *is* the way I want it. I'd rather like to have a chat with you."

Ruth's burning curiosity overcame her, mild scruples. She ran through the connecting door to Philip's flat and picked up the extension phone in his living-room.

Mrs Curtis's querulous voice was on the wire. "But what do you want to talk to me about, Mr Holt? Surely I gave you all the information you wanted this morning?"

"I want to talk about my brother, Mrs Curtis."

"Oh, but surely we discussed your brother—"

"Very thoroughly this morning. Yes, one would think we'd covered all the ground possible. And yet it seems that something slipped your memory."

"I . . . I really don't know what you mean."

"Don't you, Mrs Curtis? Tell me: why did you fail to mention that you went to Rex's room on the night he died?"

For a matter of seconds there was complete silence. Then Vanessa Curtis burst into a flurry of incoherent protestations.

Philip cut her short. "This is hardly a matter to discuss on the telephone. I'll be at the hotel early tomorrow morning."

"No ! No, don't do that . . . Not the hotel, not here."

42

"Why not?"

"It . . . it just isn't suitable, that's all. I'll have to meet you somewhere outside. At some restaurant, perhaps."

"In Maidenhead?"

"Oh no. Somewhere near, perhaps Windsor. There's a café there, near the Castle, called Hobson's Choice. Do you know it?"

"I'll find it. When do we meet?"

"Oh dear! . . . Will eleven o'clock be all right?"

"I'll be there, Mrs Curtis," he said grimly, and rang off.

Ruth replaced the extension receiver quietly and raced back to the office. Philip was eyeing her sternly.

Irritating and cheeky though she was at times, he had to admit himself fortunate in his choice of secretary. She was efficient with the paper-work and showed a promising talent on the technical side, relieving him of some of the more simple retouching and processing work. She occasionally accompanied him on his assignments and had proved herself a valuable assistant; and although their relationship was strictly a business one there was no denying that Ruth was easy on the eye and a pleasant person to have around.

He had been gathering steam for a reprimand, but when he looked at her he relented.

Then the door-bell rang.

Unsmiling, and in a tone intended to dampen her high spirits without being too severe he said quietly: "Would you have time to answer the door, Ruth?"

Chapter Five

Their visitor was Thomas Quayle, complete with carnation and small white dog.

"May one intrude in these hallowed precincts without an appointment?" Philip heard him say.

"Come on up, Mr Quayle," he called down.

As his visitor climbed the stairs behind Ruth, Philip observed him with mild interest Quayle appeared to be just about the only member of the male sex capable of climbing those stairs without being affected by the long-legged shapely vision ahead of him; when Andy or Rex had visited him Ruth had come near to demanding danger money.

"And what brings you to these parts?" Philip asked, smiling. "Do you want a portrait done – or is there some other matter you wanted to see me about?"

"*What* a very delightful place you have here," said Quayle, ignoring the question. He strolled to the bay window and gazed across at Big Ben and the Houses of Parliament "Oh, what a *splendid* view – quite beyond price! . . . No, Mr Holt, it would be an honour to be photographed by you, but in the first place, your obviously excellent work would command fees well beyond my poor pocket; and in the second place, I know of no one who would be the *slightest* bit keen to have a record of my dreary features." He stood smiling at them and stroked the little dog. "Except perhaps Whitie, eh?"

Whitie yawned hugely in his master's face, and was then allowed by Quayle to roam the office at will, dragging his lead, turning in circles, and jumping erratically till he finally upset a pile of prints overhanging the corner of Philip's desk.

Ruth quietly took charge, rescuing the prints and then giving her apparently undivided attention to petting the dog. It offered a splendid opportunity to take her mind off her work and concentrate wholly on the conversation of the two men.

". . . Why I have allowed myself to disturb you in this manner," Quayle continued, "is simply to ask if I may have my key?"

"Your key?" Philip was genuinely surprised.

"Yes, that stupid man at the hotel gave you a Yale key this morning, did he not?"

"Yes, that's right."

"He did so in error, Mr Holt. Goodness knows what the man uses for a memory. A few days ago I told him I had lost a Yale key and that he should keep a look-out for it."

Philip decided to play for time. "Yes, well . . . the key was found in my brother's room, so I suppose it's natural that Albert should have thought it was his."

"Yes, indeed, I quite realise that. Albert does not scintillate at the best of times." Quayle gave a smile and held out a limp hand. "Anyway, if you'd be so kind as to give me the key, Mr Holt, I won't take up any more of your very valuable time."

Philip hesitated for a fraction of a second before saying, "I'm sorry, I haven't got it." The smile on Quayle's thin face dissolved. "You haven't got it? What do you mean, exactly?"

"Well, when I got back here I discovered there'd been a mistake. The key didn't fit my lock, so I thought the best thing to do was to send it to your sister. I posted it off straight away."

"To Vanessa?"

"Yes, to Mrs Curtis."

Quayle stared distrustfully at him and rather sourly took out his watch, which was suspended on a gold chain. "I must say, you've been *frightfully* quick."

"I thought it might be an important key to somewhere in the hotel," Philip replied smoothly. "Anyway, there's no great harm done. Of course, I apologise for my mistake. But all you have to do is ring up your sister and get her to send it on to you."

Quayle attempted another smile, but the result was slightly warped. "As you say, that's all I have to do. Very well, I'll be tottering along. We apologise for having disturbed you." By "we" he was evidently including the dull-eyed dog now panting quietly in Ruth's lap. "Come along, Whitie," he said coolly, and, scooping up the dog, he declined Ruth's offer to see him out and descended the stairs alone.

Ruth's petite nose puckered in disgust "They'll never enter *that* exquisite creature for the Mr Universe competition!"

Philip grinned. "I should have thought it would be a nice change for you, not to have your bottom pinched by every enterprising male on those stairs."

She gave him a quick glance. "Depends on who's doing the pinching."

There was a second's uncomfortable pause and Philip hastened to change the subject. "Forgive the pun," he said, "but would this be the key to the mystery, do you think?"

"A lot of people do seem eager to lay their hands on it," Ruth agreed.

"M'm . . . Illuminating – as Inspector Hyde would say. I wonder if anyone will be willing to trade a little information in return for such a handsome-looking key?"

"It's worth a try, anyway," said Ruth hopefully.

"Yes, it's worth a try," Philip decided.

At ten minutes to eleven the next morning Philip was smoothly steering the Lancia through Windsor's narrow streets when a police constable on the fringe of a crowd flagged him down.

"Trouble up there, sir – there's been an accident. Would you mind taking the next left turning, please?"

"Certainly . . . Oh, Constable, I'm looking for a café, it's called Hobson's Choice. Can you direct me?"

"That's just about where the accident took place, sir," said the constable. "I'm afraid you'll have to park down that turning and walk back."

"What happened? Is anyone seriously hurt?"

"One fellow's been pretty badly injured, I think. Move along now, please, sir, you're holding up the traffic."

Philip took the turning the constable had indicated, parked the Lancia, and walked quickly back towards the crowd. The clanging of an approaching ambulance bell produced a reluctant gap in the throng and he caught a glimpse of a prone figure near the pavement.

A large, red-faced woman was glancing around, obviously anxious for someone to talk to. Philip smiled and she burst gratefully into words.

"I saw it happen! They got my name and address for witness. The driver musta been drunk the way he swerved about." She jerked her head towards the figure of the injured man, now being lifted carefully on to a stretcher: "Poor chap, he never had a chance. That woman was damn lucky."

"Which woman was that?"

"A woman on the pavement. She was just in front of the man that got hit. I coulda sworn she'd be the unlucky one, the way the car was going straight for her. She musta seen him coming in the nick of time – jumped like a scalded cat!"

Philip nodded sympathetically.

"Tiny little thing she was, ever so small. She'd only just got out of a car herself – that one over there. The mauve one."

Philip glanced at the Austin parked at the kerbside and felt a sharp chill of uneasiness in his veins. Urgently, he caught the woman's arm. "This tiny woman – where is she now, do you know?"

"What? Who do you mean?" muttered the red-faced narrator, flustered by Philip's abrupt manner.

"The woman who was nearly hit."

"Oh, they took her into the caff over there – Hobson's Choice . . ."

It was Mrs Curtis all right. A very pale and shaken Vanessa Curtis, resembling a startled bird which had fallen from its nest and only just avoided serious harm.

As Philip walked towards the table where she sat under the

kindly eye of a policeman she caught sight of him and gave an involuntary start, then glanced away. When he reached the table her greeting was dazed and perfunctory.

The policeman looked up. "Are you the gentleman she's expecting, sir?"

"Yes, that's right."

"I'm Sergeant Macey."

"How do you do? I'm Philip Holt."

"I'm afraid the lady's had rather a nasty experience, sir."

"So I gather, Sergeant," Philip said, and then, addressing Mrs Curtis directly, he inquired, "What happened, exactly?"

Vanessa Curtis looked evasively away, nervously twisting a handkerchief in her fingers.

Sergeant Macey answered for her. "Mrs Curtis was on the pavement, walking towards this café. A car came up at a terrible pace, completely out of control, and nearly knocked her down. Luckily she saw it in time and jumped out of the way. The chap behind her wasn't quite so quick. They've taken him to hospital."

"I gather the driver didn't stop?"

"No . . . the swine!"

"How about the number – did anyone manage to get that?" Macey nodded, and Philip thought he noticed a faint flicker of fear in Vanessa Curtis's eyes.

"Two or three different versions," Macey said. "All more or less the same, though. We'll check 'em all, one of them's bound to be right. The driver'd probably been drinking; that's generally why they won't stop after they know they've hit someone."

He glanced at Mrs Curtis and stood up. "Well, madam, if you're quite sure there's nothing else we can do for you? . . ."

"I'll be quite all right now, thank you." A trace of her habitual coyness broke through the aura of shock. She fluttered her eyelids at the sergeant and added, "Thank you for being so kind, all of you."

There was a strained silence after the sergeant had left. Someone had provided hot tea with plenty of sugar and she now pretended to be absorbed in stirring it.

"You ought to drink up before it gets cold," Philip said.

She stared straight ahead, refusing to meet his eyes.

"Would you prefer me to get you something else?" he suggested.

She shook her head. He offered her a cigarette, which she accepted, but her hand was shaking like a leaf in a storm.

There was a pause, then Philip looked at her and said quietly: "Was it an accident?"

She shot him a look of alarm. "What do you mean?"

"A simple question, Mrs Curtis. Was it an accident?"

"Yes, of course it was an accident. What else could it have been?"

"It could have been done deliberately."

"But why? Why should anyone do that?"

"To frighten you. To stop you from meeting me."

Mrs Curtis attempted a smile. "'You've got too much imagination, Mr Holt."

"Or too little. I can't imagine, for instance, just what my brother was really doing at your hotel."

"He was staying there, like any other guest."

"And just like any other guest, you went to his room in the middle of the night and had a noisy quarrel with him? All perfectly normal routine, was it?"

Mrs Curtis pressed a small white hand to her brow and muttered, "I'm sorry, I can't talk about that now. I . . . I don't feel very well."

"You told the policeman you were all right."

"Yes – well, I did feel a bit better a moment ago, but . . ."

"But now my questions have upset you?"

"Please, Mr Holt! This business of the accident has affected me more than I thought." She stood up. "If you don't mind, I'd like to go home."

Philip rose and signalled the waitress. "Very well, I'll drive you back to Maidenhead."

"Oh no! I've got my own car. I'll be perfectly all right."

Philip looked at Mrs Curtis curiously. She was a tiny,

distraught, and ostensibly helpless woman, genuinely shaken up by the accident, and had to hold on to the table for support – but there was no denying her determination to be left alone.

"Are you sure you feel well enough to drive?" he asked.

"Oh, please don't fuss, Mr Holt! I shall feel better when I get outside in the fresh air . . . If you'll just give me my key" – she held out her hand, and the gesture and tone of voice were sharply reminiscent of her brother's the day before – "I'll be running along."

"Yes, of course, the key," Philip said, beginning a pretence of searching his pockets. Vanessa Curtis watched him anxiously. "I'm awfully sorry," he said after a moment, "I seem to have forgotten it."

She gave him a look of cold fury and disbelief, then turned on her heel and marched out of the café with as much dignity as five feet two can command.

Philip ordered coffee and debated his next move. It did not take him long to reach a decision.

He left the café and set off in the direction of an ironmonger's which he had noticed as he drove into Windsor. Ten minutes later, with twin keys in his pocket, he slid behind the wheel of his car and headed south.

It was mid-week, so the roads were relatively empty, and the Lancia sped along like a sleek, feline animal.

On a straight stretch of road Philip enjoyed a short, sharp tussle with a Fiat 2300, which was a model he had once thought of buying, but the Flaminia was beautifully tuned and well able to hold its own.

It was a lovely day, the countryside looking mellow and inviting as it began to show the first hint of autumn, and despite the crushing worries on his mind he felt a surge of hope and high spirits which he could not deny.

Suddenly a crimson blur appeared in the rear mirror and, almost before he had time to identify the rival, it howled past him and disappeared round a violent bend.

"Ford Mustang, two-door hard-top," he muttered to himself. Now that was quite a car! He wondered which it was, the

200-cubic-inch Six or that fantastic V.S. – most likely the latter. It might be rather fun to have a Mustang. Of course, the Lancia had class, no one could deny that. He had felt the same about the Bentley he had once owned, but he had felt the urge for something a little more rakish and he had switched to an Austin Healey, which had been very snappy indeed! The urge was beginning to return, and when he eventually stopped to ring Ruth from a telephone booth on a quiet stretch of road near Guildford his manner was surprisingly light-hearted.

"Holt Photographs," came Ruth's bright voice over the line. "I'd like my portrait done, please," said Philip, "but I'm a two-headed monster – is there an extra charge?"

"Who's that speak— Oh, *Philip*!" Ruth burst into a chuckle of relief. "I'm so glad you're all right. I was worried."

"Worried – what about?"

"About you. Just a funny feeling I had, I know it's silly of me. What happened? Did everything go all right?"

"No, as a matter of fact it went all wrong," Philip said, reverting to his sober manner.

"Oh, Philip ! I *told* you I had a funny feeling. What's the matter – are you all right?" She sounded anxious.

"Yes, yes, I'm all right, Ruth." He gave her a brief account of the accident.

"Oh dear! First Andy and now Mrs Curtis." She was serious for once, genuinely concerned. "You will take care driving back, won't you, Philip?"

"I'm not driving back. That's why I'm ringing you. Are there any messages?"

"No. No, there's no messages. Where are you? Are you still in Windsor?"

"No, I'm on my way to Brighton."

"Brighton? Why on earth are you going there? . . . Oh, I get it!" Her inevitable enthusiasm returned. "You're calling on Mr Quayle!"

"Right, Miss Sanders!"

"But what for, Philip? Why do you want to see Quayle?"

"I give you three guesses."

Ruth debated in silence for a moment, then said: "You've still got the key . . . ?"

"Good girl! I'll bring you back a stick of rock!"

With the aid of a Sussex telephone directory which he consulted in a booth on the Hove promenade Philip was able to ascertain the address of Thomas Quayle's antique shop.

It took him some time to find it; it was in the old Regency part of the town, in a small side street leading into one of the lovely crescents.

The heavy building housing the antique shop was of less distinctive architecture, but Quayle had obviously taken pains with the ground floor and fitted an attractive bay window giving a good view of the shop interior. A fine wrought-iron staircase, screened from the street by painted railings, led down to a door in the basement.

There was no one in the shop as Philip entered, but a bell tinkled discreetly as he opened the door. The interior was surprisingly large and filled with a selection of antique furniture, paintings, porcelain, and *objets d'art*, all of it – as Philip was quick to realise – of a high quality. The prices were high too. Thomas Quayle might express distaste for "the sordid pecuniary facts of life", but he was evidently not unwilling to enjoy his share of good living.

At the rear of the shop, near an eighteenth-century sedan chair, was a small alcove giving a glimpse of narrow stairs obviously leading down to the basement.

The sound of voices floated towards Philip, and in a moment he heard Quayle and his adored white dog ascending, accompanied by a lady customer. They were deep in discussion of some potential purchase and Philip caught the tail-end of their conversation before Quayle realised that he had a visitor.

". . . I'm sure I'm safe with the jardinière," the woman was saying, "but whether my husband will agree to the Hepplewhite chairs is another matter."

"Well, if Mr Seldon is *passing*," Quayle urged, "why not ask him to drop in and take a look himself?"

The woman murmured her agreement as Quayle came into view and caught sight of Philip. For a fleeting second his expression registered shock, then he quickly mastered himself and switched on a languid smile.

"My dear Mr Holt, *what* a delightful surprise!"

The customer came into view; handsome and over-dressed. An idle woman on an eternal shopping expedition, Philip judged. She gave him a disinterested glance, determined to secure Quayle's undivided attention.

"You'll send the jardinière anyway, won't you, Mr Quayle? I couldn't bear to wait a day longer, it's just what I need for my corner table."

"Yes, Mrs Seldon, I'll have it delivered to you," Quayle answered a trifle testily.

"How soon?"

"Oh, I should be able to manage it before the end of . . ."

The woman pouted and he hastily amended his statement.

". . .You'll have it by tomorrow, Mrs Seldon, I promise you."

Mrs Seldon gave him the seal of a brilliant, satisfied smile. She was obviously accustomed to having her own way. "That will be marvellous, Mr Quayle. And I'll get Freddie to drop in and look at the Hepplewhites. Now I'm relying on you to turn all your sales charm on him – I would so like to have those chairs. Good afternoon."

"Good afternoon, Mrs Seldon."

She flashed her smile again, this time including Philip in its aura, and swept through the doorway.

Quayle bowed her out and closed the door with evident relief. "My God, the people who have money these days! . . . I'm so sorry to keep you waiting, Mr Holt. To what do I owe the pleasure of this *unexpected* visit?"

"I'm afraid I owe you an apology, Mr Quayle."

Quayle's eyebrows rose in exaggerated surprise. "Oh,really?"

The dog sniffed at Philip's trousers and he bent to pat its head, more as a gesture to win Quayle's approval than as a genuine expression of affection.

Quayle removed some copies of the *Antique Finder* from a carved oak settle and made himself comfortable in one corner, playing with the gold watch-chain that spanned his checked waistcoat. As Philip spoke Quayle watched and listened attentively; all signs of the obsequious charm he had lavished on the customer had gone.

"The last time we met," explained Philip, "I told you my secretary had posted your key to your sister in Maidenhead. I'm afraid I was mistaken. She hadn't actually done so."

"You mean she forgot to post it?"

"That's right, Mr Quayle."

"How extraordinary," Quayle purred. "She struck me as such an efficient young lady. But if I remember correctly you told me that you yourself had posted it."

Philip was slightly taken aback by the man's sharp memory, as well as the faintly ironical tone in his voice. "Yes, well . . . I was wrong on all counts. I apologise."

Quayle nodded coolly. "Won't you sit down?" He waved his hand towards a period armchair. "Try the Gainsborough, it's very comfortable."

Philip eyed the lovely piece of furniture dubiously. "May I?"

"Certainly. Beautiful things were intended to be used, you know."

"Thank you."

Thomas Quayle's supercilious manner was just beginning to irritate him. He said briskly, "I take it you still want your key, Mr Quayle?"

"Of course I do, my dear fellow! It's mine, is it not? If I came into possession of a key belonging to you, wouldn't you expect me to return it?"

"Fair enough. Now if I give you the key—"

"*If* you give me the key?"

"Yes. If I return it, would you give me something in exchange?"

"What is it you want?"

"Some information about my brother."

Quayle pursed his lips dubiously and continued to toy with his watch-chain. Eventually he said, "What makes you think I know anything about your brother? Apart from what I read in the papers? I never even met him."

"Perhaps not. Your sister knew him, though. And I'm fairly certain she knew him before he went down to Maidenhead."

Quayle shrugged his thin shoulders. "It's possible, I suppose. I don't know all Vanessa's friends, thank heaven! You can't possibly expect me to keep a check on all her boy-friends since her marital bed became lonely at night. I suggest you just return my key and then pop along to the Royal Falcon for a chat with Vanessa."

"I've already tried that. Unfortunately, your sister isn't inclined to chat – at least, not with me."

"I don't quite follow you, Mr Holt."

"It's my guess she's scared to talk."

"Nonsense ! What on earth has Vanessa to be scared about?"

"Hit-and-run drivers, for one thing, Mr Quayle. I think it's time I brought you up to date. I had an appointment with Mrs Curtis in Windsor this morning. Shortly before I arrived someone tried to kill her – someone tried to run her down with a fast car. Fortunately, they failed."

Startled, Quayle stopped fingering the watch-chain and stared at Philip. "Is this true?"

"Indeed it is. Check with the Windsor police if you don't believe me. A man walking just behind her on the pavement was very badly injured."

"How do you know it wasn't just an accident?"

"I saw your sister a few minutes after it happened. I don't think she believed it was an accident."

Quayle took out his cigarette-holder and slowly fitted a cigarette. Philip watched him closely, convinced that Quayle was shaken, despite his attempt to appear nonchalant.

"Surely it could have been a case of careless driving?"

"It could have been," Philip conceded, "but I very much doubt if it was. I'd say your sister is involved in something pretty serious and that her life is in danger."

There was a long pause, during which Quayle appeared reluctantly to make up his mind. "What exactly is it that you want to know?"

"Was my brother a friend of yours?"

"I knew him slightly."

"You'd met him before he went down to Maidenhead?"

"In a manner of speaking, yes."

"Why didn't you mention this before, Quayle?"

Quayle produced an elegant silver lighter and slowly lit his cigarette before replying. "What difference would it have made? I didn't kill your brother, I promise you that, Mr Holt. I should leave things as they are, if I were you. Playing the super-sleuth won't help."

"I want to know whether or not Rex committed suicide, and I intend to find out!"

The response was long in coming but when it came there was no doubting its authenticity.

"He was murdered."

As Quayle spoke the shop bell tinkled and to Philip's extreme annoyance Mrs Seldon swept imperiously into view. "I'm so sorry to disturb you again, Mr Quayle, but I've decided to risk my husband's disapproval and settle for the Hepplewhite chairs before someone else snatches them away."

Quayle managed to force a weak smile but did not rise.

"Very well, Mrs Seldon, I'll have them delivered along with the jardinière."

"Thank you so much." She beamed brilliantly at him, as a teacher might treat a recalcitrant child who has suddenly done well. "I wonder . . . do you think I might just take another peep at them?"

Quayle sighed and slowly unwound his length from the oak settle. "Very well, Mrs Seldon . . . I shan't keep you a minute," he added to Philip as he led her towards the basement, the dog following at their heels.

While they were gone Philip wandered idly about the shop, looking at the various pieces for sale. His eye was taken by a magnificent mantelpiece of Italian marble, the massive shelf supported by two gilt caryatids. Near by he noticed a large chest with a superb Canaletto painting of St Mark's Square, Venice, reproduced on the lid. Ideal for storing some of his vast stock of prints and negatives, he thought. However, it bore a large label marked SOLD, so he was obliged to dismiss the idea. He turned from the chest to admire some delicate Wedgwood and Dresden figures, but could not really give his mind to any of them. His nerves were taut with concentration on the statement Quayle had just made, and he cursed Mrs Seldon for interrupting just as the antique dealer had seemed about to talk. Would Philip still be able to persuade Quayle to tell the truth, or would he have regained his composure after the diversion and refuse to enlarge on the subject? Philip could hear the woman chattering in the basement, and Quayle's occasional monosyllabic comments.

To quell his rising tension he lit a cigarette and looked around for an ashtray. He spotted an innocuous glass bowl which did not appear to be a period piece standing on Quayle's small working-desk and crossed over to it.

It was then that he saw the book.

Sonnets and Verse by Hilaire Belloc was perched negligently against an ivory book-end, next to bound copies of a monthly art magazine. He picked up the book with trembling fingers and rapidly leafed through the pages. Then he heard Mrs Seldon coming up the stairs and was obliged to slip it quickly back into place.

". . . No, there's no need to wrap it, thank you," she was saying as she came into view beyond the alcove.

"It would be no trouble, no trouble at all," Quayle's voice answered from below.

"No, no, I wouldn't hear of it! I want all my neighbours to be jealous when they see what a treasure I've found."

She carried an intricately wrought Regency jardinière about the size of a large candlestick, and was clutching it as though she had purloined the Crown Jewels.

"You won't forget the chairs, will you, Mr Quayle?" She called "Goodbye!" over her shoulder, and beamed at Philip as he held the shop door open for her.

He sighed with relief as she swept out into the street, and waited for Quayle to appear. As nothing happened after a moment or two he took a chance and stole quickly over to the slim volume of poetry on the desk. He flicked through the pages, but found nothing unusual. He examined the binding and had started to look through the pages again when he was startled by the ringing of the telephone on the desk.

He pushed the book back into place, stepped quickly to the other side of the shop, and pretended to be immersed in a scrutiny of the Canaletto reproduction on the lid of the chest. Hearing sounds of movement from the basement, and the dog's excitable whining, he expected at any moment to hear Quayle ascending the stairs. But there was no sign of him. Eventually the telephone ceased to ring and the shop was plunged into a silence disturbed only by the ticking of a grandfather clock.

A suspicion of uneasiness crept through Philip's veins. He went to the top of the stairs and called out.

There was no answer. The silence was so tangible he felt he could almost reach out and touch it.

Cautiously he descended the stairs.

At the foot was a large padded door covered in expensive green leather and studded with gold buttons. Quayle evidently liked peace when he was in his private den.

Philip tapped on the door, received no answer, tried the handle, and pushed it open.

He entered a thickly carpeted room – private den had been a good guess, this was obviously the purpose of the room. But Quayle was nowhere to be seen. He had been there, Philip could see; he had apparently rummaged swiftly through some papers on the opened-out flap of an eighteenth-century bureau in one corner, and left a confusion of letters, files, and invoices strewn about. But he seemed to have left through another door which opened on to the iron staircase outside leading from the basement to the street.

Philip's first instinct was to go after him. He was profoundly anxious to hear more from Quayle. He started towards the outside door, then changed his mind; Quayle had evidently left some minutes before and would hardly be waiting in the immediate vicinity. Instead, Philip took a quick look through some of the confusion of papers in the bureau.

As he took hold of a large envelope the wrong way up a sheaf of photographs slid through his fingers and scattered over the floor.

Two familiar faces stared up at him from the shining prints . . . multiple replicas of Sean Reynolds and his accordion-playing wife – every one of them kith and kin to the single photograph in whose existence Inspector Hyde had refused to believe . . .

As he stooped to pick up the prints he was startled by the report of a powerful exhaust as a throaty sports car started up and roared away. There was a screeching of tyres as it took a corner far too fast. Throwing open the outside door Philip raced up the steps and into the street.

A faint blue wisp of exhaust smoke drifting in the mote-filled air was all that remained of the frantically driven car. The road was empty except for his own car parked at the kerb. He lit another cigarette and strolled thoughtfully towards it, undecided as to his next move.

An object dangling from the closed lid of the Lancia's boot caught his eye as he moved closer.

The gold chain glinted in the sunlight, far more brilliantly than when it had so recently lain across Quayle's waistcoat in the gloom of the antique shop . . . Philip wrenched open the boot and was just quick enough to catch Quayle's slumped body as it keeled over – a knife buried to the hilt between his shoulder' blades.

Chapter Six

Inspector Hyde sat in the visitor's chair, conscious of the fact that he was not particularly welcome.

Inspector Bertram Lang, in charge of the inquiry into the murder of Thomas Quayle, was a hearty, heavily built young man, ruddy of complexion and rather overbearing of manner; it was quite clear that he had no doubts about his own efficiency and resented the Scotland Yard man's "interference".

"Holt's our man, I think you'll find, Inspector," he said, leaning back at a dangerous angle in his tubular steel chair. "There's not a shadow of doubt about the fingerprints on the handle of the murder weapon."

"Ah yes, the knife," said Hyde quietly. "What does Mr Holt have to say about that?"

Inspector Lang snorted. "Rather a thin explanation, I'm afraid. He says he grabbed at the body to stop it falling out of the car, and by sheer bad luck he grasped hold of the knife. Frankly, I don't believe it."

Hyde pursed his lips but made no comment

Inspector Lang tilted forward so abruptly that the steel chair crashed on the floorboards. "As for opportunity, Holt had all the time in the world to go about it in that murky shop. He admits that himself. After that customer left, all Holt had to do was slap the knife into Quayle, bundle his body into the car, which he'd very conveniently parked near the basement, and drive off."

"But he didn't do so," Inspector Hyde pointed out in mild tones. "Instead, he phoned London and asked me to come down at once, and then he telephoned the local police here."

"Bluff! Sheer bluff! The fellow got cold feet about driving around in a car with a corpse, so he invented this cock-and-bull story about people nipping into the basement, hitting Quayle over the head with a convenient blunt instrument, and then sticking a knife into his back. Frankly, I don't believe it!"

Hyde remained silent.

"Besides, Quayle's got a perfectly good name in this town; there's no earthly reason why anyone should want to murder him. He wouldn't hurt a fly. Holt, on the other hand, seems to be rather a suspicious character."

"Why do you say that, exactly?"

"Well, you've told me yourself he's pretty deeply mixed up in the Maidenhead suicide – a dubious alibi and a tidy little inheritance as a result of his brother's death. Add that to the fact that he's been pestering Quayle's sister, and then the curious reasons which he says brought him down to Brighton . . . Well, it's as plain as a pikestaff that the fellow's after something."

"I'm inclined to agree with you there."

"Well, there you are, then! Whatever it was that Holt wanted, Quayle either didn't have or wouldn't give him. So Holt loses his temper, there's a fight, and Bob's your uncle!"

Hyde took out his tobacco pouch and began placidly filling his pipe, trying not to notice the acutely dangerous angle at which Lang was again tilting his chair. "I admit," he said cautiously, between puffs, "that things look somewhat black for Mr Holt at the moment. As you say, we have only his word for it to account for what happened in the antique shop, and there are certainly some very strange factors which he hasn't been able to account for. Nevertheless, I never believe in making up my mind too soon in these matters . . ." He struck a match and concentrated on his pipe, while Lang scraped his chair and made impatient noises in his throat. "Inspector Lang – I wonder if I might ask . . . I should appreciate it very much if I could have a few words in private with Mr Holt. Could that be arranged, do you think?"

Lang sniffed sceptically. "As you wish – if you really think you can get something out of him which we haven't been able to."

Hyde, blunted the barb by giving Lang a pleasant smile. "One can always try, I think. Is there any word from the murdered man's sister?"

Lang glanced at his watch. "She should be here at any moment, I should think. Will you want to see her in private too?"

"Oh no, that shouldn't be necessary. By the way, forgive me for mentioning it, but you *are* making a very thorough search of Quayle's shop, I take it?"

"Of course!" Lang affirmed irritably. "We're not *all* thundering amateurs down here, you know!"

Philip Holt was giving an account of his eventful day, and Hyde listened carefully.

"The Inspector in there didn't get the point of the key," Philip said with exasperation. "I trust its significance hasn't escaped you too?"

"Its possible significance, let us say. You had, in fact, made up your mind to try and barter it for information?"

"That was the rough idea."

"I see. And Thomas Quayle was just beginning to loosen up when his customer came back. Now was that chance, do you think?"

"I thought so at the time, but now I'm not so sure. It's my opinion that she actually stunned him with that hefty jardinière. I doubt if she would have knifed him – but someone else could easily have done that, and then carried the body out to the boot of my car."

"But you heard him talking to Mrs Seldon, didn't you, sir – while she was coming up the stairs, you said!"

"Yes, I did, Inspector. At least, I thought I did – but it must have been someone imitating his voice, just to fool me."

Hyde tapped out his pipe and said musingly, "Yes, yes, but this is all pure speculation, of course."

"There's simply no other explanation! Good God, Inspector, I was talking to the man five minutes before he was murdered! What other explanation could there be?"

Hyde shook his head. "Beware of finding an explanation too soon, Mr Holt. Some things are best left on the side to cool."

"Such as the book, for instance?"

"Yes. And these photographs of the soldier, and his wife."

"Well, at least you now know I didn't make that up. They're all more or less the same, reproductions of the one Rex showed me."

"Yes, I follow," Hyde answered as he studied the photographs which had been Philip's main purpose in asking him to come down from London.

"Incidentally," Philip said, "the last time we met you said you were going to visit Andy Wilson. Did you see him, Inspector?"

Hyde nodded.

"How is he? What did he say?"

"He didn't say very much, I'm afraid."

"Why? Is he still too ill?"

"I think he'll pull through all right, Mr Holt. But I got the impression he doesn't feel like talking to me."

"I wonder if he'd talk to me?"

Inspector Hyde considered the idea. "It's possible, sir." He tossed the prints on to the table and said after a pause: "It's a pity you touched the knife."

Philip 'sighed. "Don't I know it! As soon as Lang started mentioning fingerprints I knew I was in for trouble. A blind man could see that I needed Quayle alive, so he could go on talking! If I'd wanted to stab him in the back with a knife I'd have worn gloves."

"Only if it was a premeditated action, Mr Holt. Inspector Lang is inclined to think that you may have acted in a fit of temper."

"Inspector Lang is a—" Philip began hotly, then broke off as a police sergeant entered the room.

"Inspector Lang's compliments, sir," he said, "and he thought you'd like to know that Mrs Curtis has arrived."

"Ah, thank you, Sergeant. I'll be right along."

The interview that followed in Bertram Lang's office was a source of mild amusement to Inspector Hyde. Had Mrs Curtis come to

Brighton alone, all would have been plain sailing for the Sussex police officer; she was, however, accompanied by her manager, Douglas Talbot, and within a short space of time Talbot and Lang had met head-on like two obstinate mules on a narrow path.

Although Lang pointedly addressed his questions to Mrs Curtis, who sat white-faced with shock and seemingly incapable of grasping the harsh reality of her brother's death, it was Talbot who provided the answers in his commanding voice.

"Look here, Inspector, I'm sure Mrs Curtis would like to get back to Maidenhead as soon as possible," he said aggressively, "so if you could keep the questions down to a minimum . . ."

"I'm afraid you'll have to bear with me a moment or two longer, Mr Talbot," Lang answered, equally aggressive. "Now, Mrs Curtis, you tell me you've never heard of Mrs Seldon, and you don't know why your brother had those photographs or the book of poetry?"

"She has already told you—" Talbot began.

"Mrs Curtis?" Lang insisted, directing a quelling look at Talbot.

The frail woman blinked at him and shook her head. "No, Inspector. The photographs are a complete mystery, I've never seen those people before. As for the book – well, there's nothing really strange in Thomas possessing a volume of poetry, you know. He was an intellectual, he loved all things to do with the Arts."

"Yes, Mrs Curtis," Hyde interposed in a gentle voice, "but you do realise, don't you, that it was the same book of poetry that Rex Holt was studying when he stayed at your hotel? Doesn't that strike you as rather an odd coincidence?"

Vanessa Curtis lifted her hands helplessly and made little dancing movements with her fingers.

Talbot dived into the silence. "Look, gentlemen, far be it from me to tell you how to run your own show" – Hyde winced and Lang glared at the interruption – "but has it never occurred to you that perhaps poor old Thomas knew nothing about the photographs and the book?"

"What exactly do you mean by that?" Lang challenged him.

64

"Is it not true that you were told about them by Holt *after* Thomas was murdered?"

"Yes, that is true."

"Right! Then isn't it possible that Holt is lying? Holt can say what he likes, Thomas isn't here to dispute his word. Isn't it possible that he brought these dubious articles down from London himself and planted them?"

There was a flicker of interest in Hyde's eyes. "That is just possible, Mr Talbot. But for what reason should he do that?"

"Ah," said Talbot, tapping the side of his nose with a long forefinger, "now you're asking me to read Holt's mind. I rather think that's your job. All I'm saying is that a fellow like Holt needs watching or he'll pull the wool over your eyes."

"Could you be a little more explicit, Mr Talbot?" Lang put in.

"Well, if you want me to spell it out for you, Inspector, Holt is a damned liar!"

"Indeed?"

"Yes. At the Inquest he said he was surprised to learn that his brother was staying at the Royal Falcon."

"Go on," said Hyde quietly.

"It's my opinion that he knew all the time that his brother was in Maidenhead. He's simply, trying to bamboozle everybody! He knew perfectly well what his young brother was doing at the Royal Falcon."

"And what was he doing there, Mt Talbot?" Hyde inquired.

"I only wish I could tell you that, gentlemen. You'd better ask Holt"

Lang, who had been craning forward with an eager expression, let out an explosive snort of annoyance. "This is only supposition. You've nothing definite to go on, have you?"

Talbot smiled complacently and waved his forefinger again. "Let us say it's supposition based on fact."

"What fact?" Lang barked.

"The fact that by a strange coincidence Philip Holt happened to be friendly with someone who was staying at our hotel at that time."

"Who was that?" Hyde asked quickly.

"A certain gentleman from Hamburg – Dr Linderhof," Talbot announced importantly, and smiled smugly at them like a conjuror who has brought the rabbit out of the top hat.

Inspector Lang looked puzzled, so Hyde briefly explained, then turned his deceptively mild gaze on Talbot. "Can you prove what you've just said?"

"Yes, as a matter of fact I can, Inspector! Shortly after Rex Holt committed suicide Dr Linderhof made a telephone call. I . . . er . . . I accidentally overheard part of it. You must realise that as manager it is part of my job to know what is going on in the hotel, officially and unofficially – it's the only way to retain complete control, you understand."

In other words, you were eavesdropping or listening in at the switchboard, Hyde thought dryly.

"I didn't know then to whom Linderhof was speaking," Talbot went on, "but when the name Rex was mentioned two or three times I naturally picked up my ears."

Lang grunted. "Go on."

"Linderhof made an appointment to see the person he was speaking to. When the call was over I discreetly checked with the switchboard and got the number he'd been ringing. It was a Westminster number, that of Holt Photographs Ltd."

There was a short silence, eventually broken by Hyde. "Why haven't you told us about this before?"

The hotel manager shrugged his shoulders. "I didn't really see at the time that it could be important. It's only now, in the light of Holt being mixed up in this shocking murder of Thomas Quayle, that it strikes me as being possibly significant."

"You know, Mr Talbot," Inspector Lang began officiously, "withholding vital information from the police is—"

Talbot held up an arresting hand. "Inspector, we've all heard that little tag before. What does it, in fact, amount to? Try and give the police a helping hand with an intelligent theory and you get told to mind your own business. They seem to know the lot."

Lang flushed with anger, but Hyde slipped in imperturbably:
"Not quite the lot, sir."

"Hyde speaking. Anything new, Sergeant?"

He was using the special telephone in his car, as he drove back to London, to talk to Sergeant Thompson.

"Yes, sir. Some interesting progress on the Sean Reynolds photograph at last."

"Is that so! Splendid! Incidentally, that Reynolds photograph seems to play some kind of role in the murder of Thomas Quayle – the dead man's bureau was littered with copies of it. Now, what have you to tell me?"

"We've found the couple who posed for the picture, sir."

"Good!"

"Needless to say, their name isn't Reynolds."

"Who are they?"

Sergeant Thompson gave him the full details and was amused to hear his Chief whistle.

"Illuminating – very illuminating."

"Yes, isn't it? I expect you'll be calling on Mr Philip Holt again in the near future, won't you, sir?"

"The answer, Sergeant, is in the affirmative."

Chapter Seven

Ruth Sanders in a bikini was quite a sight.

Inspector Hyde caught a glimpse of her through the studio door as Philip greeted him in the office the following morning. She was reclining on a low sun-seat before a brilliantly lit backdrop of palms and deep blue Mediterranean.

She grinned at him impudently and called out, "Hello, Inspector! Sorry I couldn't answer the door, Mr Holt said I wasn't decent."

"It would have been a nice surprise," Hyde said, blushing slightly.

Philip rather irritably made to shut the door on Ruth, but the Inspector seemed in no hurry to seal off the charming view.

"I didn't know your secretary also acted as a model?"

Philip scowled. "She doesn't, as a rule. I've got a professional model coming in this morning for a suntan lotion ad, and we generally save time by getting the shot lined up in advance – lighting and all that sort of thing."

Ruth slipped nimbly from the sun-seat and, lighting a cigarette, struck an impudent pose. "I'm just a poor neglected stand-in who will never see herself on the cover of *Vogue,*" she said.

"Ruth, for Pete's sake—"

"Mr Holt doesn't usually allow me to pose in costume."

She waved deprecatingly at the two strips of red-and-white polka-dotted cloth which clung to her body. Then she added, "I thought it was high time he realised that other girls besides these snooty fashion models have decent figures."

"You mean indecent," growled Philip. "Put that robe on if you insist on standing there chatting shamelessly with the Law."

Ruth gave a mischievous grin and slipped on a white beach-coat. It just reached to her hips and was, if anything, more disturbing than the previous vision.

"Now, *if* you've quite finished . . . ?" Philip said.

"Not quite," Hyde answered amiably. "Just one question, if I may, Miss Sanders. Were you in the office when Mr Quayle called here?"

"Yes, Inspector."

"Do you happen to remember what he was wearing?"

"Yes, I think so . . ." She screwed up her brows and considered. "He had a light-weight coat with a velvet collar . . . a dark blue suit . . . a carnation in his buttonhole . . . and he had a little dog. Whitie, I think he called it."

"I see. Thank you."

The Inspector appeared satisfied, so Philip reached forward and shut the studio door with marked emphasis.

Hyde strolled to the bay window and admired the view. "You really are a very lucky man, Mr Holt. There must be innumerable people all over the world who would give their eye-teeth to have a view like that."

"That thought is brought home to me rather poignantly each quarter when I pay my rent."

"Yes, I don't imagine they exactly give it away." Hyde turned from the window and took out his pipe and pouch. "Well now, I trust you're feeling a little rested after your strenuous day yesterday?"

"As rested as a man can feel when he discovers for certain that his brother was murdered, and is then nearly arrested on a murder charge himself."

Hyde nodded and started to fill his pipe.

"I suppose I owe you a vote of thanks," Philip continued. "If you hadn't put in a good word for me I'm damn certain Inspector Lang would have clapped me in jail for the knifing of Thomas Quayle."

"Inspector Lang – is an ass," said Hyde flatly, striking a match.

The remark was so unexpected, so out of keeping with the man's normal ultra-cautious habits, that Philip burst out laughing.

69

"That's a purely private opinion," Hyde added hastily. "I trust it will remain within these four walls."

"It will," Philip promised.

As Hyde began puffing on his pipe and tamping it down to make sure it burned evenly Philip stood up and paced the room. "Inspector, I'm at my wits' end! Where do we go from here? I thought the possession of that key might literally unlock some doors for me; but Mrs Curtis was too frightened by the car accident to talk, and her brother had only just got started on an explanation when he was . . . eliminated. I'm absolutely determined to get to the bottom of Rex's murder, but I can't for the life of me see where to try next."

Inspector Hyde blew out a cloud of smoke and suggested, "Corporal Andy Wilson, perhaps?"

Philip looked at him and saw that he was in earnest. "Well, that seems to be a logical step, I agree. It's obvious he knows something about the matter; but I'm surprised you haven't been grilling him yourself."

"I have. Before and after the attempt to shoot him."

"And he won't talk?"

"Not to me, he won't. The mere sight of a police officer seems to close him up like a zip-fastener. But it's possible he has something to tell you. He asked if you were likely to be dropping round to see him again, and I took the liberty of promising you'd call this evening."

"Right, I'll do that. I'm glad to hear he's up to receiving visitors?"

"Yes. As a matter of fact, he had one yesterday: Luther Harris, the music-shop owner."

Something in the Inspector's tone of voice made Philip look at him sharply. "There's nothing odd about that, surely?" Hyde made no comment.

"They were very good friends, the three of them," Philip said. "Rex, Andy, and Luther. They often used to visit Luther's shop when they were on leave."

"Yes, Pop's Corner; I remember your telling me. Has Luther Harris been to see you, Mr Holt?"

"No. But he wrote me a very nice letter of condolence on Rex's death."

"I see. Well, you'll let me know how you get on with Corporal Wilson, won't you?"

"Yes, of course."

Philip imagined that the visit was at an end, but Hyde strolled towards the chair where he had deposited his briefcase and began rummaging in its contents. "There are just two more points I want to discuss with you, sir, then I'll be on my way." He took out several copies of the mysterious Sean Reynolds photograph. "It's just possible that we're making headway on this little puzzle at last, Mr Holt. But I want you to take another look at these pictures."

Philip frowned. "All right, Inspector, I'm looking."

"You don't know these people?"

"No."

"You haven't the slightest idea who they could be?"

"Not the slightest."

"You're quite, quite sure?"

"I've told you a hundred times, I haven't the faintest idea what the joke's all about."

Hyde hesitated a moment, then seemed satisfied. Putting the photographs into his briefcase he went on speaking, though his tone was slightly cooler than before. "My other point, Mr. Holt, is that you've told me on several occasions that you've no idea what your brother was doing at Maidenhead."

"That's correct."

"Surely there could be a very simple explanation? That he went there to see a friend of yours."

"A friend of mine?"

"Yes. Dr Linderhof."

Philip looked really astonished. "Whoever told you that Linderhof was a friend of mine? Apart from the Inquest I've only met the chap once in my life!"

"When was that?"

"Er . . . the day before yesterday."

"Where?"

"Well, as a matter of fact he came here, to the studio."

"Don't you think it would be a good idea if you told me about it, Mr Holt?" Hyde said coldly.

Philip was annoyed at being put on the defensive, but he tried to keep anger out of his voice as he gave the Inspector an account of Linderhof's visit.

Hyde sat bolt upright as he listened to the story of the heated quarrel between Mrs Curtis and Rex Holt which Linderhof had overheard from the bathroom at the Royal Falcon. "Why the dickens didn't Linderhof tell that to me!" he exclaimed impatiently.

"Because he's in trouble back home," Philip explained. "He comes up before some Medical Tribunal in a few days time, and he wanted at all costs to stay out of the limelight. That's what he came to England for – the peace and quiet. The last thing he bargained for was getting mixed up in a British murder case."

"Nevertheless . . ." Hyde began, then sighed heavily. "If only people would be a little more honest and open with me."

"Then you'd be out of a job, Inspector."

Hyde smiled ruefully. "You mustn't imagine I should mind that too much, sir. Well, I'll be on my way. No, please don't bother to come down, I'll let myself out."

That evening, at the end of a busy day in the studio, Philip went to the Middlesex Hospital where Andy Wilson was recovering from his shot wounds.

As elder brother, and for all purposes guardian to Rex, Philip had never been very enthusiastic about Rex's choice of friends, and Andy Wilson in particular had rated low on the list. He considered Andy to be the wrong kind of influence for an easily-led person like Rex. He had not, however, been able to do anything about it.

The meeting between the two men in the long, forbidding public ward was not a success. After the first platitudes about the sick man's health had been exchanged, there were large gaps of awkward silence in their conversation. From time to time Philip tried to pin Andy down, to extract some useful piece of truth from him, but each time Andy veered away like an obstinate mule.

"Look, Andy," Philip burst out in exasperation, "you more or less asked me to come and visit you! You've got something on your mind, a blind man could see that! Out with it, for Pete's sake! If you don't know why you bothered to pinch that book of poetry from my studio and you have no idea who took pot-shots at you at the Elephant and Castle, what *do* you know?"

Beads of sweat were gathering on Andy's scalp beneath the thin yellow hair. He avoided Philip's eyes as he eventually said, "I just wanted to warn you, mate, that's all."

"Warn me? Whatever for?"

"You're sticking your neck out too far. Look what happened to Rex. It wasn't suicide . . . he was murdered."

"Is that a guess or an informed statement?"

"It's not a guess."

"And do you know who did it?"

"No. And if I did I couldn't tell you."

"Why not?"

"I just couldn't, that's why."

Philip grunted in disgust. "I fail to see why you think it necessary to warn me."

"Look, mate, d'you want the same treatment as they gave Rex and me? 'Cos you'll get it if you don't stop interfering."

Philip's tone was ice-cold as he answered, "What would you suggest? That I go quietly home and forget the whole business? That I give up trying to find out who murdered my own brother?"

"That's the ticket, mate! Unless you're tired of life."

Philip sighed heavily. "Someone's been putting the fear of hell into you, Andy!"

The sick man attempted a show of indignation. "You ask my mates – Andy Wilson don't scare easy. But this is something different, this is big league we're playing in, these people are real desperate . . ." His voice trailed off into a hoarse whisper and from his corner bed he glanced uneasily at his nearest neighbours, who were fortunately several empty beds away.

"What do you mean, these people are desperate? Who *are* these people?"

73

Andy shook his head, and Philip had to bend closer to catch his reply. "I don't know, and if I did I wouldn't say. Why don't you just drop the whole caper and—"

"Listen! Get this into your head, Andy! I'm going through with this business, right to the end of the line. I'm not stopping until I've found out what Rex was mixed up in and who murdered him."

"You'll live to regret them words, mate," Andy assured him, then added, "Or maybe I shouldn't say live; it might come out the other way."

Angry with frustration and bewilderment Philip drove home through the darkening streets, uncertain whether it was even worth while telephoning Hyde in view of the meagre harvest of the interview.

Big Ben was striking eight o'clock as he garaged the Lancia and strolled towards his front door. For no particular reason he happened to glance up at the windows of his flat; what he saw sent his pulse-rate soaring . . .

Apparently he had visitors.

But they seemed a little shy about using the electricity; they seemed to prefer the use of a flashlight.

Just for a moment he remained quite still, debating what he should do. It would, of course, be prudent to call the police and tell them he had burglars, but this was not the moment for prudence. While he was making the phone call, his unannounced visitors might leave, and he was curious to know just who they were.

He opened the street door and crept up the stairs. With infinite care he slipped the key into the lock of the office door and let himself in.

It was just possible, in the gathering gloom, to make out the familiar outlines of Ruth's desk and other pieces of furniture. He put one ear to the door which led to his flat and listened intently. Then he quickly dived for cover behind a large filing cabinet.

High heels beat an assured tattoo along the passage. Two seconds later the door was opened and the beam of a torch probed the room. He could not see who was holding it, but the footsteps had been those of a woman, and a moment later an elusive but faintly familiar whiff of scent reached him. Then the outline of a woman silhouetted against the window showed itself. She was tall and completely self-assured. Philip thought he could guess her identity.

He remained crouched behind the filing cabinet to see what she was after. She held her torch with one hand and with the other began rifling through the drawers of Philip's desk. Then she tackled the desk where Ruth worked.

Philip was not a very tidy person, but the chaos which the bold female intruder was causing would have driven Ruth mad. He decided he had waited long enough. His hand glided up the wall and snapped on the electric light switch.

"Wouldn't you prefer a little more illumination?" he said. The woman swung round, dazzled by the light, and uttered an unlady-like expletive.

"Why, hello, Mrs Seldon! Looking for some choice antiques? You won't find any Sheratons or Hepplewhites here, I'm afraid."

He had to hand it to her, she was a remarkably self-possessed customer. In a matter of seconds she had recovered her composure and again resembled the idle woman on an eternal shopping expedition – though perhaps a lady who finds herself unexpectedly locked up in the bargain basement after nightfall might have been a more apt description.

"What are you looking for, if I may ask? Perhaps I can help you."

Her eyes seemed to bore through him, expressing utter contempt; then suddenly she glanced beyond his shoulder as though she had seen someone behind him.

"Fletcher! " she called imperiously.

Philip grinned and did not bother to turn round. "Sorry – you'll have to do better than that. They've retired that gag long ago."

"Are you sure?" said a harsh voice behind him.

Philip whirled round and saw a tall, thin, saturnine figure in a belted raincoat standing in the passage, partly hidden by shadow.

"Okay, Clare. Get out!" the man snapped.

With complete composure Clare Seldon switched off her torch, slipped it into her handbag and, without giving Philip so much as a glance, stalked past him and descended the stairs.

The tall figure stood with his hands in the pockets of his tightly belted raincoat, a smile on his ill-shaven face.

"Who the devil are you?" Philip said.

"Ask no questions and you'll be told no lies, Mr Holt."

"Well, what the hell do you want?"

"The key. Just the key, that's all."

"What key?"

"Don't waste my time."

"Oh, you must mean the one Mrs Curtis . . ."

A thin-bladed knife shot out like the forked tongue of a snake in the man's right hand. "Give!" he snarled.

Philip managed a smile. "Sorry, chum, no can do. I've handed it in to the police. Inspector Hyde has it. Why don't you call on him?"

The man called Fletcher gave a laugh. "I dare say you did. We'd still like to have the one you kept, though."

"What the hell do you mean?"

"When you left the café in Windsor you went to an ironmongers and had a duplicate made. I know what I'm talking about, so quit stalling! Let's have that key!"

Philip tried to conceal the fact that he was inwardly stunned by this revelation. It had never entered his head that anyone might have been shadowing him in Windsor. His thoughts raced.

Unless he was mistaken the ball was still in his court. They wanted the key, it was still in his possession, and he was quite willing to exchange it for a fair bargain. Previously he had tried to barter it for information; now the only chance left was to exchange it for a man – Fletcher. And preferably Fletcher without his knife.

"You're being rather stupid, aren't you? Do you imagine I walk around with the key on me?" he said.

"Why not? Seems a likely place to me. Turn out your pockets!

And let's skip the funny stuff, shall we? I might be tempted to try out my new knife."

"What's the matter, did you leave the old one between Thomas Quayle's shoulder blades?"

It was only a guess, but it was a logical one and seemed to strike home. Fletcher's eyes narrowed and he swore violently.

Philip obligingly emptied his pockets. Cigarette lighter, silver cigarette case, handkerchief, loose change, and a small penknife fell to the floor – then his key-ring, enclosed in a small leather holder. Fletcher pounced on this, and after a brief examination tossed it away.

"I told you I hadn't got it on me," Philip said truthfully. "Okay, so you've hidden it. Where? In the teapot, I suppose?"

"It's over there," Philip said, gesturing towards his desk. "All right. Get it! But remember . . ." he added, switching the flick blade in and out with menacing swiftness.

Philip walked slowly over to the desk. On it stood several box-files packed with prints of various advertising photographs. A handsbreadth away was the telephone. He glanced over his shoulder and made as if to grab the receiver, but instead he snatched up a box-file and pressed it to his chest, whirling round in a lightning movement just as Fletcher hurled the knife.

The knife thudded into the box-file. Philip flung the box at Fletcher and caught him a winging blow on the head as he made a dive for the stairs. Philip managed to catch Fletcher by the belt of his raincoat, but he wheeled and lashed out with one foot. The foot struck Philip in the pit of the stomach and he fell backwards in crushing pain, but just managed to get a grip on Fletcher's ankle as he tumbled over.

A wild struggle followed. The pain in Philip's stomach was almost overwhelming and he had to gasp for breath as he scrambled to his feet. Fletcher struggled free and yanked a drawer from Ruth's desk, crashing it into splinters on Philip's skull.

Dimly he felt himself losing consciousness and was scarcely aware of Fletcher's footsteps thumping down the stairs and the slamming of the street door.

He was not sure whether it was a matter of seconds or minutes before the ringing of the telephone penetrated his numbed brain. He struggled to his feet and reached for the receiver.

A bright, familiar female voice was saying something unintelligible.

"Who's that? Stop shouting . . . Oh, it's you, Ruth!"

"Philip, what's *wrong?*" she shouted.

"I . . . I seem to have got a crack on the head . . ."

"Stay where you are, I'll be right over!"

Half an hour later Ruth was solicitously bathing the cuts on his forehead and deftly applying sticking plaster.

"Are you feeling better now, Philip?"

"Yes, I'm okay, Ruth."

Ruth smiled. "We won't be able to enter *you* for the Mr Universe competition."

Philip managed a grin. "Instead of all this female chatter and Florence Nightingale routine, why don't you fix me a stiff drink?"

"May I make it two?" she said. "This business has shaken me up almost as much as it has you."

"Go right ahead."

She went through to his flat, and in a moment she was back with whisky, glasses, and a soda siphon. He watched as she poured out two stiff measures, and realised that he was inordinately glad to see her.

Ruth handed him one of the glasses and murmured, "Cheers."

"Cheers! Here's to my next meeting with Master Fletcher. I knew I guessed right about his being a nonentity without his knife."

"That was a shocking risk you took, Philip," she said reproachfully.

"I had to get him to throw the knife. I felt certain I could handle him once he was unarmed. It seems I overestimated my ability."

"They ought to give you a medal for taking him on in the first place." Ruth set her glass down and began to tidy up some of the disorder in the office. Suddenly she let out a squeal of excitement. "Hey, what colour is your wallet?"

"M'm? Brown pigskin. You've seen it often enough on pay day."

She was scrambling on the floor underneath his desk. "That's what I thought. Now you have two. Mack-the-Knife seems to have dropped his during your fight."

She emerged with a greasy black wallet in her hand. The initials C.F. were stamped on one corner in fading gilt.

"C.F.? F for Fletcher, I wonder?"

"It must be!"

Philip took the wallet and held it pensively in the palm of his hand. "You know, we should really hand this over to Inspector Hyde, shouldn't we?"

Ruth gave him a look, took the wallet, and emptied the contents on to her desk. "My female curiosity won't hold out that long."

The harvest at first seemed meagre: three five-pound notes, several pound notes, a betting slip, some dubious postcards of Parisian origin, five grubby membership cards to obscure Chelsea drinking clubs, and a dance ticket.

"Horses, sex, booze . . . that makes sense," Ruth mused. "But I don't quite see how this ticket to a dance in Camden Town fits, into the picture."

"Let me have a look." Philip held out his hand. He read out the-details from the simple piece of pasteboard.

*"Wednesday, September 29th. at 8.30 p.m. Gala Dance
in aid of the United Services Hostel. 12/6d.*

I doubt if Fletcher ever wore a uniform in his life."

"With broad arrows on it, perhaps?"

"Wait a moment! There's something familiar about the date of that dance. Wednesday, September 29th. Rex did say he was going to a dance with Andy, didn't he? Yes, don't you remember – he said he'd be back from Ireland by then and didn't want to miss it?"

"Come to think of it, I believe he did say something about a dance. I think he was hinting that he wanted me to go with him."

Philip tossed the card back on to the desk. It fell face down and for the first time they noticed faint writing in pencil on the back.

Ruth seized it and read out: *"Rex Holt – Andy Wilson – Luther Harris.* Well, what do you make of that? Just three names, nothing else."

Philip snatched the card. "As Inspector Hyde might say, this could prove illuminating."

"But what can it possibly mean?"

"I don't know, but I'm damn well going to find out! Make yourself glamorous on the 29th, Ruth. You and I are going to have an evening out."

Chapter Eight

The big poster outside the dance hall in Camden Town announced that "Monty Fry and his Frymen" would be "frying tonight". From the wave of sound that shredded the warm evening air and met them in a blast as they entered the vestibule it was clear to Ruth and Philip that Monty and his boys had already been cooking for some time. The vestibule was packed with servicemen and their girl-friends, and Philip had to use his elbows to get anywhere near the cloakroom, where he eventually succeeded in depositing their coats.

As they had only one ticket it was necessary to buy another from a sexy-looking blonde who stood behind a trestle-table nearby.

"Can I interest you in tickets to our raffle as well?" she asked Philip, leaning forward to display a generous expanse of well-supported frilly blouse. "It's all in aid of the United Services Hostel. The raffle only costs seven-and-six."

"In for a penny, in for a pound," said Philip. "I'll take one."

"And one pound it is!" said the blonde cheerfully, handing him the admission to the dance and a stub of raffle tickets to choose from.

Ruth was eyeing some photographs on the wall behind the table, depicting, a young blonde singer, with a striking similarity to the sales-girl, hanging on to a microphone.

"What are the prizes?" Ruth asked cautiously.

"First prize is a Hi-Fi set, that one over there, worth a hundred quid. Second prize is a record-player, and consolation prizes are signed copies of my sister's latest L.P."

"And who is your sis—" Philip began tactlessly.

Ruth nudged him sharply and indicated the photographs. "It's Muffet, of course! Her latest record's Number 3 in the charts."

"Oh . . ." Philip murmured, but further comment was cut short by a burst of ecstatic screaming coming from the entrance, in which the young girl behind the trestle-table joined with apparent enthusiasm.

Ruth and Philip turned to see a teenager in a long Empire-line dress with trumpet sleeves attempting to force a way through the crush. There were shrieks of delight from some of the younger people in the vestibule and a small rush for autographs; but it was not this spectacle of mid-twentieth-century hero worship which intrigued Philip so much as the shrewd, porky man with rimless glasses with whom Muffet had made her entry. It was Luther Harris.

"Well, well, well!" Philip murmured.

"Is that Luther Harris?" said Ruth unbelievingly. "I wouldn't have recognised him in that rig-out. Still, I don't suppose I've met him more than two or three times. He looks as happy as a dog with two tails."

"Wouldn't any man with a girl like that on his arm?"

"He'll be had up for baby-snatching if he's not careful. She can't be a day older than fifteen."

"That's where the money lies these days, my dear. Every time little Miss Muffet opens her mouth somebody will pop a ten-pound note into it. Luther's merely moving with the times, latching on to his own private pop singer."

Ruth glanced at the Hi-Fi set and the pile of long-playing records with a picture of the young singer in full colour on the glossy cover. "He'll be in on the sale of her records and probably the equipment too."

Philip nodded as the noisy centre of interest moved slowly towards the table where they were standing. "That certainly explains his presence here, anyway. He'll be pretty surprised to see us, though. Here they come."

There was a scene of welcome between the sisters, and Luther

Harris rapidly fired questions concerning the evening's financial success. For a second he seemed to catch sight of Philip, then his eyes sped nervously away and a moment later he began to steer his young protégée away towards the dance hall.

"Luther!" Philip called in a clear voice.

There was no mistaking the reluctance with which Luther stopped and slowly turned. He screwed up his face and produced an unconvincing expression of surprise and pleasure.

"Hello, Philip, old sport! Never expected to see you here."

"Put it down to Ruth's account. She's crazy about dancing," said Philip glibly. "You remember Ruth, don't you?"

Luther extended a podgy hand and smiled vaguely. "Er . . . yes, you came into the shop with Rex once, I seem to remember."

"That's right."

Muffet eyed Philip and Ruth with swift assessment, and rejecting them as being of no particular use to her she muttered, "You'll find me with Monty," and drifted away.

"Terrible thing about Rex, Philip," Luther said. "I was shaken rigid."

"Yes. Thank you for your nice letter. I'd have replied, only . . ."

"I understand, old sport." He glanced nervously about him, then signalled to his protégée's retreating form. "Be with you in a sec, dear. You'll excuse me, won't you?" He made to go. Philip cut in quickly, "Perhaps we could join up later, Luther, when you're not so busy? I'd like to have a talk with you."

"Oh . . . yes. Well, you see . . . it's a big evening, you know, and . . ."

"Say about ten-thirty? I expect there's a bar here, isn't there?"

"You bet there is," Muffet's sister supplied from behind them. "On the first floor. All profits in aid of the—"

"Right. See you there, Luther. Okay? Ten-thirty, don't forget."

"Well . . . I'll try and manage it. So long."

They watched him trot smartly in the wake of his protégée.

"He didn't seem wildly enthusiastic about meeting us, did he?" said Ruth as they edged their way towards the blast of sound coming from the bandstand.

"Far from it. I think he'd have cut me dead if I'd let him get away with it"

"Perhaps he's just embarrassed about meeting you – I mean on account of Rex having died. People do feel awkward at times like that; they just don't know what to say."

"Perhaps. Anyway, we'll find out. Let's search for a few square feet of dance floor, shall we? We've got to do something to while away the time until ten-thirty."

Ruth glared at him. "You sure won't win any prizes for gallantry, Mr Holt. I know a lot of young men who'd give their eye-teeth for the chance to dance with me."

Philip coughed uncomfortably and took her gingerly in his arms.

"If you come about two yards closer, I'll bite you," she said with heavy sarcasm.

As things turned out, they need not have worried about how to fill their time until their appointment with Luther Harris. Chance had something very interesting in store for them.

Shortly before ten o'clock there was a roll of drums from one of the Frymen and the traditional "*touche*" of cymbals which subdued the noisy crowd to relative silence. A pink spotlight picked out Monty Fry on the bandstand. In a stentorian voice he announced that the Star of Stage, Screen, Radio, and Television, the Great Little Mullet, was going to sing, after which she had agreed to draw the tickets for the raffle and present the prizes.

The young girl proved to have a reasonably pleasant voice, almost totally without talent; but, supported by the crushing power of astute publicity, good orchestration, and a powerful microphone, the public gullibly accepted the implication that they were being entertained by a highly talented star.

It was when she had finished her act that the evening suddenly snapped into significance for Philip and Ruth. The winning raffle tickets were drawn and the winners were asked, amidst a roll of drums, to come up to the dais to accept their prizes.

The Hi-Fi set went to an R.A.F. sergeant who, cheered by his companions, stepped sheepishly up on to the spotlit stage with his girl-friend.

Then the second prize of the record-player was drawn. "Ticket Number 183. Norman Stansdale. Would the lucky winner step up here please? . . . Norman Stansdale . . . Number 183 . . ."

A shout went up in one corner of the hall and a red-faced soldier stood up, beaming with pleasure, and grabbed his wife by the hand.

"Look!" hissed Ruth, clutching Philip's arm in tremendous excitement. "It's the couple in the photograph! Sean Reynolds and the woman with the accordion!"

"Good God, you're right! Stansdale, eh? Now who the devil are they?"

Amidst loud cheers the soldier and his wife mounted the platform and stood grinning foolishly in a brilliant spotlight. "I'd give my eye-teeth to have Inspector Hyde beside me now," Philip said tensely.

"And I'd give more than that to win one of those consolation prizes and get up there alongside them," Ruth added.

But their luck was out. Six consolation tickets were drawn and Philip's number was not among them. Ruth sighed with despair.

Then Philip said suddenly, "I've got an idea."

He threaded his way through the crowded hall towards the vestibule. The blonde with the generous bosom was just in the act of packing up her belongings at the trestle-table.

"I say, are any of those long-players of your sister's still for sale?"

"That's the general idea."

"Good! I think she's great! I'll buy one."

In a moment he was back at Ruth's side, clutching the record.

"This should do the trick. We'll pass ourselves off as fellow winners – Private Stansdale will be far too bemused with all that flapdoodle up there to notice who actually won consolation prizes."

The ceremony over, Monty Fry and his Frymen leapt into action once more and within seconds the dance floor was filled. Philip did not let the Stansdales out of his sight. When they left the floor and appeared to be heading in the direction of the bar, Philip nudged Ruth and they followed discreetly in the couple's wake.

There was a vacant corner table in the bar, from which they were able to watch the soldier and his wife as they bought drinks for a boisterous group of Army friends and toasted their good fortune. Philip was prepared to wait. He needed to be able to talk to the couple on their own, and he knew that his approach had to be casual and as natural as possible.

The entry of Luther Harris seemed to throw a temporary spanner into the works.

Luther caught sight of Philip and a shadow of nervous worry crossed his face.

"Hello, Luther. So glad you could make it. Sit down and have a drink."

Luther hesitated, then took the proffered chair. "Can't stay long," he muttered, glancing anxiously over his shoulder. "Muffet's got one of her migraines, says she wants to be taken home early."

"Great little singer you've got hold of there, Luther."

"H'm? Oh yes. She's good for business."

He took out a silver cigarette case and lit a cigarette with nervous hands. Suddenly remembering his manners he offered the case to Ruth and Philip. Both declined.

"Are you sure?" Luther said. "You used to smoke like a chimney."

"I'm trying to give it up."

"Oh." He drew deeply on his cigarette. "Well, what was it you wanted to see me about?"

"Oh, I just thought it would be nice to have a chat, that's all," Philip said blandly.

"I see."

An awkward silence followed. Philip was convinced Luther would feel obliged to break it.

"Terrible news about Rex. I just couldn't believe it."

"I *don't* believe it, Luther," Philip said emphatically. "Ugh? How do you mean?"

"Rex didn't commit suicide. He was murdered."

Luther licked his lips rapidly. "Is that what the police think?"

"It's what I think."

"Yes, well, if I were in your shoes I'd probably think the same – especially after what happened to Andy. That was a rum do."

"It certainly was. Do you think it had something to do with Rex?"

"Looks mighty like it. It's too big a coincidence, otherwise. Those boys were mixed up in something, Philip. They must have been. God knows what it was, though."

Luther sipped his drink and glanced rather obviously at his watch.

Philip said hurriedly, "I understand you've been to see Andy at the Middlesex?"

"Yes, I popped in for a chat the other day. 'Chat' is a bit of an exaggeration – I didn't get more than a dozen words out of him."

"It was the same when I called. Tell me, Luther, did Rex mention at any time the notion of going down to Maidenhead?"

"Not that I remember. What was he doing there, anyway?"

"Nothing – except reading a book."

"Rex reading a book! He must have turned over a new leaf. What was the name of the hotel?"

"The Royal Falcon."

"Is that the one just before you get to the bridge?"

"No, it's over the bridge, on the other side. Lovely old place – half-timbered, thatched roof, and a history dating back to the old coaching inn days. It's owned by a woman called Vanessa Curtis, but she has a manager, a man called Talbot."

"I've never heard of either of them, old sport."

"No, I don't expect you have. How about a chap called Fletcher, though – have you ever heard of him?"

Luther took off his glasses and rubbed them energetically, appearing to consider the question. Eventually he replied, "No, I don't think so."

Philip raised his eyebrows. "Funny. He's heard of you."

Luther seemed to stiffen. "What do you mean?" he asked cautiously.

"He broke into my studio the other day, and we had a slight punch-up. He doesn't know it, but he left me a souvenir of his visit

– his wallet. Inside it was this ticket." Philip produced the pink card of admission to the dance. "It's got three names scribbled in pencil on the back. Rex Holt – Andy Wilson – and Luther Harris. Odd, isn't it?"

Luther reached out and snatched the ticket. His fingers were trembling as he studied the pencilled names. When he started to speak his throat seemed to be dry and he took a quick drink before going on. "Why the devil should my name be on this?' "I don't know, Luther. I was rather hoping you'd be able to answer that."

"But I've never heard of anyone called Fletcher. What did he look like?"

"He was tall, thin – rather badly shaven. He had a belted blue raincoat and handled a knife rather smartly."

Luther took another quick gulp of his drink. "A knife?"

"Yes. He threw one at me."

Luther attempted a weak smile. "Well, at least he missed."

"No, as a matter of fact, his aim was darned good." Philip gave a brief description of the fight at his studio.

Luther wiped his brow, which had suddenly broken out in a sweat-rash. "This is incredible. I mean . . . Well, anyway, I've never heard of this chap, and I certainly haven't the faintest idea what my name is doing on that ticket. What's Andy got to say about the whole thing?"

"I haven't asked him."

"Why ever not?"

"Because it wasn't till after I'd seen Andy at the hospital that Fletcher called on me."

"Well, if I were you, I'd show Andy this ticket and ask him if he knows Fletcher. And while you're about it, find out what my name is doing on the ruddy thing!"

"Fair enough, Luther, I'll do that."

Luther stood up. "I must be hopping it or Muffet will give me hell. So long, old sport. Goodbye, Ruth."

Philip watched with doubt and speculation as the man waddled away. He turned to ask Ruth for her impressions of the conversation, only to find that she had slipped away from the table a moment before. He caught sight of her heading for the Ladies Powder Room, clutching the long-playing record Philip had bought. He looked swiftly across to where Stansdale was sitting, and grinned to himself; the soldier's wife had evidently gone on the same errand.

Philip lit a cigarette, his first that evening, and waited patiently for the two girls to emerge. They were a long time, but as the door to the Powder Room eventually opened he could see that the ruse had paid off. Giggling together over some feminine secret, the two girls made their way in a flush of new-found friendship towards his corner table. Philip stood up.

"Philip, this is Freda Stansdale," Ruth announced, "the lucky winner of that record player. I told her we hadn't got a gramophone, so she's promised to let us play our consolation prize on her new set."

They all laughed and Philip said, "Congratulations on your superior luck."

Freda Stansdale smiled ruefully. "Fat lot of good the thing's going to be to us, unless we sell it. Norm's always on the move, in the Army, and we haven't got the cash for storage."

"I should sell it, then. Why don't you ask your husband to come over and have a drink with us – maybe we could find you a buyer."

Mrs Stansdale considered the idea and seemed to like it "I must say I wouldn't mind getting him away from that mob," she said with a jerk of her head, indicating the boisterous circle surrounding her husband. "Hang on a tick and I'll fetch him."

When she had gone Ruth whispered quickly, "What do we do now?"

"Play it by ear," Philip murmured.

In a moment Freda Stansdale returned with her husband. They settled round the table while Philip ordered drinks. At first the conversation consisted mainly of jocular references to the prizes they had won and the number of pints it had already cost Norman Stansdale to celebrate.

"Having a good leave, are you?" Ruth asked with her warm smile.

"I'll say I am!" the soldier replied. "Trouble is, I go back Friday, worse luck!"

His wife cut in good-humouredly, "Don't let him kid you, he loves the life. He's glad to see the back of me."

Stansdale winked heavily at Philip and raised his tankard. "To sweethearts and wives – may they never meet"

As Philip smiled and raised his glass to the toast Ruth addressed him across the table. "Friday . . . wasn't that the day poor old Rex was due to go back?"

Philip caught on swiftly. "Yes, I believe it was." He added casually to Stansdale, "Ruth's talking about a friend of hers – he was on leave like you. Only the Army will never see him again. He committed suicide a little while back. You probably read about it in the papers."

"Not that soldier in the hotel at Maidenhead?" Freda exclaimed.

Ruth nodded soberly. "Yes. Rex Holt. A wretched affair."

"And he was a friend of yours?" asked Norman Stansdale, wide-eyed with surprise.

"Yes," Ruth replied. "A very dear friend."

"Well, I'll be blowed! Talk about a small world!"

"Why?" asked Philip as calmly as he could. "Did you know him?"

"No, but I've met his brother."

Philip gulped at his beer and Ruth began hunting in her bag for cigarettes in order to cover up her emotions.

"Fancy that," said Philip casually. "Where did you meet him?"

"At his studios. He's got a nice little pad not far from Westminster Bridge. He took some pictures of the Missus and me a few months ago."

Philip managed to say, with perfect composure, "Rex's brother took some pictures of you? Are you sure? What's the photographer chappie's name?"

"Philip Holt," replied Stansdale amiably. "A funny to-do it was, right from start to finish. Freda and I never really understood what it was all about, did we, old girl?"

Freda giggled. "No, but we understood the fifty quid all right. That bit made sense."

"It sounds intriguing," Ruth said. "Tell us about it, won't you?" Thank goodness they're both a bit merry from the beer, and the excitement, she thought, or they'd surely put two and two together and see through us !

Happily for them, Freda Stansdale was the chatty type and needed little prompting. The story she told, with frequent interruptions from her husband, was indeed "a funny to-do from start to finish" and it was only by the use of the utmost self-control that Philip and Ruth avoided giving themselves away as they listened.

"It was last February, just towards the end of Norm's leave."

"We was skint. Proper skint," Stansdale put in.

"Dead right, we were. Don't think we had more'n ten bob between the two of us. We was having a beer in the pub in the Strand, when this dark-looking smoothie comes over and gets talking. Said his name was Cliff Fletcher and he wanted a couple of faces for a publicity photo – said he worked for a big advertising agency or something."

"I didn't like the smell of it at first," Stansdale confided as he gazed owlishly into his tankard. "Thought this feller was trying to get Freda to pose in the altogether. But he said I had to be there too, and all he wanted was our faces for this photo. He offered us fifty quid for the job. Well, like I said, we was proper skint, so we hummed-and-ha'd a bit, but we pretty soon said yes."

"This smoothie gave us his card with the address of a photo studio on it" Freda Stansdale took up the story again. "It was this place of Philip Holt's over by Westminster Bridge we was telling you about We promised to be there at ten o'clock the next day. Norm and me had a good old chin-wag about it that night, I can tell you, but in the end we decided we couldn't come to much harm, and the money sounded real nice."

"And you did get paid as promised?" Ruth asked.

"Oh yes."

"What sort of pictures did they get you to pose for?"

"Daft, they were – proper daft!" said Stansdale. "Might have been more fun if they *had* got Freda to pose as Eve." He winked heavily at Philip. "You might not think it but she's not got a bad—"

"Norm!" his wife said warningly, at the same time giving him a good-humoured jab in the ribs. "That's enough of that, young man! Keep the party clean." She turned to Ruth. "Men!"

"They're all the same," Ruth cheerfully agreed. "Tell us about the pictures."

"Well, like Norm says, they were proper daft. I was made to strap an accordion round my shoulders. Norm had to stand behind me and grin at the camera, while I was supposed to be concentrating on the keys. I can't play a note, so you can guess I felt pretty soft, sitting there with that thing in my lap. I got used to it after a while, though. They took scores of pictures, all more or less the same; the only difference was they made me put my hands in different positions on the keys."

"And it was Philip Holt himself who took these photographs?" Philip asked.

"Yes."

"Was anyone else there?"

"Only this bloke Fletcher. He sat on one side and gave sort of advice and instructions with the help of a bit of paper."

"A piece of paper? Whatever for?"

"Norm and I never did get the hang of that. Every now and then they'd stop, while we was baking under the big lamps they use, and they'd get their heads together over this bit of paper the smoothie was holding. Then they made me alter the way I was putting my fingers on the keyboard, and take some more pictures. Real queer it was."

"And that was all there was to it?"

"Yes, that was all."

"What sort of a man is Philip Holt?" Ruth asked innocently. "Is he anything like his brother? I expect you saw Rex's picture in the papers."

"Hard to say, really . . ."

Philip had an uncomfortable moment when Freda's eyes rested

92

on him steadily for a moment as she considered the question. He stared downwards at Muffet's picture on the record sleeve, glad for once that there was no striking resemblance between himself and his younger brother. Ruth had addressed him as "Philip", but the Stansdales would obviously accept this coincidence; if they recognised a family likeness, however, they might become suspicious and fail to answer any more questions.

"No, not much likeness on the whole, I should guess," Freda said at last.

"Rex was tall," Ruth prompted daringly. "Tall and fair, and very good looking."

"Was he?" Stansdale shook his head. `Well, they weren't much alike, then – though the photographer brother was tall enough, wasn't he, Freda?"

His wife nodded but did not seem very interested in this aspect of the story, and although it was immensely frustrating neither Philip nor Ruth dared press the point any further.

"What happened then?" Ruth asked.

"That's about all there was to it. At the end of the day they paid us and we left. Haven't seen either of them from that day to this. Once my leave was over I forgot the whole caper."

"Did you ever see any of the photographs they took?"

"Not at the time, no."

"But you've seen them since?"

"Yes, I have. Funny thing it was. Happened just a few days ago. I was down at Aldershot, visiting a couple of pals there – hadn't seen them in ages. We was playing darts in the local when in walks this civvy, and after a chat with the barman he comes over and shows me some of them photos. Never been so surprised in all my life, I can tell you!"

"Go on."

"Well, he started asking me where the pictures were taken, how much we was paid, and all the rest of it. So I naturally says what the hell has it got to do with him? He just grins and shows me his badge of office, like. Scotland Yard! Gave me a hell of a fright it did. But he told me I didn't have nothing to worry about, it was just a routine inquiry and all that. I don't see that we did anything wrong, do you?"

"What? . . . Wrong – no, of course not," said Philip distractedly. "Very sensible of you to pick up an easy fifty quid like that; I wish someone would make me the same offer. Well, dear," he said, glancing at his watch and addressing Ruth, "it's getting late. I think we ought to be on our way. It's been nice meeting you," he said to the Stansdales. "I hope you enjoy the rest of your leave."

They shook hands all round and Philip went to fetch their coats.

Ruth met him in the vestibule. "What now?" she asked tensely.

"There's a certain gentleman called Hyde I'd like a word with," Philip said grimly.

"You're sure it was the Inspector who found Stansdale in the bar at Aldershot?"

"Hyde or one of his assistants. Either way, it's an appalling situation! One can't blame Stansdale and his wife for being taken in by some impostor, but if I don't hurry up and destroy Inspector Hyde's illusions he'll slap a warrant on me before you can say Jack Robinson!"

"Why hasn't he done so already? He must have known about this for several days."

He probably likes playing cat and mouse. I've simply got to reach him and clear myself."

They had come out into the street and Philip made for a convenient telephone box. Ruth waited outside.

A minute later he came out of the box, pale with anger and worry. "Damnation! He refuses to see me tonight. Says he's quite sure it can wait till tomorrow."

"But what did he say about—"

"He wouldn't let me get a word in edgeways. Talk about cat and mouse! I really think he's enjoying himself. He said he'll drop round to the studio at eleven tomorrow morning. Never known him so casual and disinterested. I really don't understand the man!"

"It's a difficult sex," murmured Ruth.

Chapter Nine

The meeting between Inspector Hyde and Philip the following morning was a stormy one. Ruth, who was not officially present but had been rather careless about fully closing the office door, told Philip afterwards: "You sounded like a thoroughly naughty schoolboy who's either in trouble for something he's done, or worse still for something he's *not* done."

Things got off to a bad start when Philip's opening salvo was: "Inspector, what the hell are you playing at?"

Hyde was quite imperturbable. "Could you be a little more explicit, sir?"

"You know what I mean. I'm talking about the Reynolds photographs – or to bring things up to date, the Stansdale photographs. The last time you came here you showed me the wretched things for the umpteenth time and asked me if I knew the couple."

"That's right, Mr Holt; and you told me you didn't."

Philip exploded with a burst of suppressed air, "Good grief, man! – And all the time you were one hundred per cent certain that not only did I know them but that I actually took the blasted photographs right here in this studio!"

"Was I convinced of that, sir?"

"Well, of course you were – you must have been!"

Hyde smiled amiably. "Very well, then; let me ask you again, did you take those photographs?"

"No, I didn't! But I can't expect you to believe me when—"

"Why not, Mr Holt? I'm really not such a doubting Thomas. If I were, there are at least five aspects of this case which would have given me grounds for suspicion, if not actual grounds for arrest."

"Five? I suppose you wouldn't like to stop being so cagey and tell me what they are?"

Hyde took out his pipe and thoughtfully filled it. To an impartial observer it would have been obvious that he was giving Philip time to cool down. He hunted for his matches and slowly lit the pipe.

"All right, Mr Holt, why not? It might help you to repose a bit more confidence in me if I remind you of some of the times when I've taken a trusting view of your . . . frequently bleak situation. Now let me tell you the history of the Rex Holt case so far – as seen through an official microscope."

"This should be interesting," said Philip thinly

"Well, to begin at the beginning, with your brother's death . . . The textbooks tell us that the first things to look for are Motive and Opportunity. You had the opportunity to murder your brother because – by your own admission – you happened to be a few miles away on the night of his death. I sifted your alibi very thoroughly and I eventually came to the conclusion that you were telling the truth."

"That was very nice of you."

"Nevertheless, as alibis go, it was decidedly shaky. The fact remains that you *did* drive down to Marlow to judge that, competition, and you *could* have slipped into the Royal Falcon on your way back. You *could* have shot your brother, faked a suicide note, and slipped out of the hotel in the confusion and noise of the Dramatic Society's banquet. You and I know that it wasn't what happened, but if you're fair-minded you must admit that it *could* have taken place."

"It's physically possible," Philip agreed grudgingly.

"Thank you. Now, when I showed you the note at your brother's bedside you said it was definitely in his handwriting."

"I admit it took me in. It looked exactly like Rex's writing. But it couldn't have been – Rex was murdered!"

"Precisely. The experts have since proved that it was a very clever forgery."

"I see."

"And who forged it, Mr Holt? Who would be in a better position to concoct a clever imitation of Rex Holt's hand than his brother, who'd known him all his life? And couldn't your adamant statement that he had written that note have been a determined effort on your part to make me believe just that?"

"Good God, Inspector, you're surely not suggesting—"

"I'm not suggesting anything, Mr Holt," Hyde said soothingly. "I'm just giving you the story as seen through the official microscope, remember?"

"I follow you. Go on, Inspector."

"Now we come to Motive, the most important factor in any murder case. Who stood to gain by your brother's death? At first showing, only one person – you. The sum of twenty thousand pounds left in Trust for him automatically became yours when he died a few months before he could inherit."

"Someone must have known all this and tried to plant—"

Hyde held up one hand to impede Philip's flow. "I am simply telling it as it appeared, or might have appeared. A large sum of money was thus diverted into your hands. I naturally asked myself – did you need it? Things began to look really black for you when I found out that the answer was yes. Very badly. Your business had gone through a shaky passage and you'd built up a formidable total of debts. Your divorce was costing you a pretty penny in alimony each year—"

"Dammit, man, I admitted all this!"

"I know you did. But that didn't alter the facts, which we would have found out sooner or later anyway. Now then . . . ." Hyde seemed for a moment unaccountably embarrassed. ". . . Er. . . . please forgive my next point – but it *could* be deduced that monetary gain was not your only motive in wishing to get rid of your brother. There was also the delicate matter of Miss Sanders."

"Ruth? What the devil did she have to do with it?"

"Please don't excite yourself; I repeat, this is pure hypothesis, although perfectly sound reasoning. From various inquiries and observations we gleaned that Miss Sanders, at one time was quite friendly with your brother; and I'm inclined to think, whether you care to admit it or not, that you're quite fond of her yourself, Mr Holt."

Philip flushed a deep red: "Look here, Inspector . . . my relationship with my secretary is nothing more than a business one. She's a very nice girl, but—"

"I'm sorry, you must excuse the clumsiness of my phraseology, and I really don't mean to intrude into your private life; but I'm a policeman, engaged on a murder case and I must continue to examine every possible detail. It could be inferred that in getting rid of your brother you were also eliminating your main rival for Miss Sanders' affections."

"Preposterous! Miss Sanders is just a very efficient secretary—"

"Then you must be blind, Mr Holt; she's very much more than that. However, to proceed. The fourth item concerned the Sean Reynolds story. Imagine my feelings when, after energetic research by a big team from the Yard, no evidence could be found to substantiate any of the story you told us. No soldier named Sean Reynolds in Hamburg – no street accident – no widow in Dublin – and no photograph or wallet among your brother's possessions. I didn't like it at all."

"I dare say not; but how about when the photograph eventually turned up?"

"That only added to the mystery. I only had your word for it . . . The manner in which it suddenly appeared in the showcase, to which only you and your secretary had a key . . . I think I can be forgiven for feeling very uneasy about the matter."

"You've had enough suspicions to arrest me ten times over!"

"Yes." Hyde stood up, smiled, tapped out his pipe, and strolled to the bay window. "But happily I'm not a very impulsive man, Mr Holt."

He turned round and paced the room for a moment or two.

"I prefer to act on facts, not hunches and suspicions. For example, I could have drawn some dubious conclusions from the Wilson shooting incident. He was shot soon after leaving this studio, and you did admit to having left the premises yourself for a breath of air. I don't think anyone would have suggested that you climbed into a car, shadowed Wilson on his pub crawl, and shot at him at the Elephant and Castle – but you could easily have used an outside telephone to arrange for it to be done. And it would have been possible for you to slip that volume of poetry into Wilson's bag before he left."

"The thought never occurred to me."

"I'm sure it didn't. Nevertheless, it was possible. And again, I was none too happy about that phrase Wilson used in his delirium, telling you to destroy the photograph."

Philip shook his head like a punch-drunk boxer struggling for consciousness. "I wonder you didn't put my picture up on the hoardings with 'Public Enemy Number One' under it, Inspector. You've even been kind enough to miss out a few additional facts, such as Linderhof's secret visit here, and Mrs Curtis being nearly run over outside the café where I arranged to meet her, and, of course, Quayle's murder with my finger-prints on the knife."

Hyde smiled enigmatically. "Then there was the surprising truth about the accordion photographs. I was really astonished when Sergeant Thompson told me he'd succeeded in running the original models to earth, and that they'd told him they posed for Philip Holt in his studio in Westminster! Indeed, I had a very worrying time until inquiries proved that you couldn't have taken those photographs because—"

"Because I was in Bermuda in February."

"Exactly!" The Inspector went over to a chair where he had deposited his briefcase, and produced an envelope with some notes scribbled on it "You arrived in Bermuda on February 2nd and left on the 28th. You stayed at the Ocean Beach Hotel and occupied Suite 102."

For the first time that morning Philip's features relaxed into a pleasing smile. "You don't appear to have found out what I ate for breakfast, Inspector."

Hyde chuckled. "I expect we could manage that, if necessary." He pushed the envelope back into his briefcase. "Now then, Mr Holt, I trust that this little chat has cleared the air between us, and that we'll be able to be perfectly frank with one another in the future."

"Yes, indeed. You've been most forthright."

"Then supposing you return the compliment and tell me how you happened to be attending that Gala Dance at Camden Town last night? As you see, we're still keeping ourselves posted about your day-to-day movements."

Philip gave a cough of embarrassment. "I . . . I had a little argument the other evening with a man called Fletcher. I found him searching my flat. He threw a knife at me – there was a bit of a struggle, and he left in rather a hurry. He didn't find what he came for, but afterwards I found his wallet on the floor. There was a dance ticket in it with the names Rex Holt, Andy Wilson, and Luther Harris written on the back. Rex had mentioned he was going to this dance so I thought it would be a good idea if I went along myself. I took Miss Sanders to make it look more natural."

Inspector Hyde's eyebrows had risen into huge arcs. "And you accused *me* of being cagey and holding out on you, sir! Don't you think you should have told me about all this a little sooner?"

Philip grinned. "We've only just made our treaty of mutual co-operation, Inspector."

Hyde sniffed. "Well, I could read you the Riot Act about with-holding information from the authorities, Mr Holt, but I trust you've got the message by now. Supposing you give me the details about Mr Fletcher and this 'little argument'."

Philip complied, and took pains to leave nothing out of his ac-count. Hyde listened in rapt silence, then examined the knife in the box-file which Philip took from a cupboard.

"You were remarkably lucky, sir. I don't think I've ever heard of a box-file saving a man's life before. Have you touched the handle?"

Philip shook his head. "His prints should still be on it."

"Good. And did you get a good look at this man Fletcher?"

"Yes. I'd recognise him again if I saw him."

"That helps." Hyde took a notebook from his briefcase. "Give me a physical description, will you?"

Philip did so, and then the Inspector asked, "You don't happen to have the dance ticket as well, by any chance?"

"Yes. I only had to show it to gain admission, I didn't have to hand it in. Here it is."

"Thank you. The ticket itself is unimportant, but it might be illuminating to have the handwriting on the back analysed. And you went to the dance on the hunch that it might prove interesting?"

"Yes. Also I was curious about Luther Harris's name being linked with the other two."

"Was he at the dance?"

"Yes, indeed. He was practically the organiser. He seemed to be sponsoring some young pop singer."

"Yes, we know about that. Did you show him the ticket?"

"Yes. I think it shook him, but I can't say we learnt very much. I'm not even sure if he knew of a knife-throwing type named Fletcher, but I did get the impression that he got the wind up a bit."

"I can imagine," Hyde commented dryly. "You say Fletcher and this woman from Brighton, Mrs Seldon, were ransacking your flat in search for the key. They must have been very annoyed when you told them you'd handed it in to the police."

Philip gave a guilty cough. "Unfortunately they were very up-to-date with their information. I had a duplicate key made and they knew about it."

Hyde frowned. "That was a curious thing to do, Mr Holt."

"Yes, but I was convinced the key was of vital significance – too many people were trying to get hold of it, so I thought a duplicate might come in handy. Also, I'm still not entirely convinced that it didn't really belong to Rex."

"I can put your mind at rest there. Mrs Curds claimed the key was hers and proved it by locking and unlocking the door of her private apartment with it. Of course, she might possibly have given it to your brother, for one reason or another?"

The mild insinuation in the Inspector's remark was clear, but Philip shook his head. "Rex was a bit of a lad with the ladies all right, but I fancy Mrs Curtis was a little too old for his tastes."

"I'm inclined to agree with you." The Inspector glanced at his watch and stood up. "I must be going. By the way, you haven't told me how you got on with Wilson at the hospital."

"Not at all well. Silent as the grave, except for some silly nonsense about warning me not to poke my nose into this affair."

"To which you replied . . . ?"

"That I intend to go on poking my nose in until I find out who murdered my brother."

"As my young son would say," Hyde commented with a fond chuckle, "Them's fightin' words', Mr Holt. I'm very glad to hear them; we need all the help we can get and I don't mind admitting it. However, remember that I'm paid to take risks, and you're not. If you see Mr Fletcher or Mrs Seldon coming down the street, cross quickly over to the other side and give me a ring. I'll be very glad to make their acquaintance."

"I'll remember that, Inspector."

The two men shook hands, and Hyde descended the stairs and let himself out.

As the front door closed Ruth appeared in the office. There was a strained, flushed expression on her face which Philip could not immediately explain. She said in a taut voice, "May 'just a very efficient secretary' remind you of your appointment at eleven-thirty to photograph that model at Charing Cross Station?"

He looked at his watch. "Lord! I must hurry! Which model is it? I've forgotten her name."

"It's not one of your glamour girls this time, Mr Holt – it's a model train."

"Oh, heavens yes! Well then, I shall want the Hasselbind, film, spare bulbs, tripod, the Weston Master—"

"All packed, ready and waiting, *sir*," she said icily.

"Good girl." The indignation in her tone penetrated at last. "Ruth, just how much of that conversation did you overhear?"

"Enough."

"Look, Ruth—" he began, but the ringing of the telephone cut him off. "Oh, never mind, I'll have to explain another time. I'm not here, I've already left!"

He snatched the heavy bag of equipment which Ruth had prepared for him and started down the stairs two at a time.

He had just reached the front door when Ruth called down to him, "Aren't you at home to Luther Harris? He says it's urgent."

Philip retraced his steps and took the phone. 'Luther? . . . Why, what's up? . . . I'm just going out on a job . . . All right, if you think it's that important I'll meet you somewhere . . . Charing Cross Station . . . Main line . . . In about an hour? Okay, near the book-stall, but you may have to wait. See you." He hung up.

Ruth asked swiftly, "Something to do with last night?"

"Could be. Says he's got something important to tell me about Rex. I'm off. Don't forget to lock up if I'm not back by lunch-time."

"You forget: I'm a *very* efficient secretary, Mr Holt."

Philip met Luther Harris near the book-stall on Charing Cross Southern Region station, having completed the photographing of the model locomotive.

"What's on your mind, Luther?"

Luther glanced nervously around at the slack midday traffic on the concourse. "Look, old sport, couldn't we talk somewhere private – your car, for instance?"

"Very well."

Luther was silent as Philip concentrated on the tricky job of navigating a passage through the mesh of traffic in Trafalgar Square. They drove under Admiralty Arch and down the broad sweep of the Mall till a suitable quiet spot alongside the park offered itself. Philip pulled in to the kerb.

A Ford Mustang, this time a cream-coloured convertible, flashed by and momentarily took his mind off Luther Harris. He wondered how much he would get for the Flaminia in a trade-in.

"Philip, are you listening?" said the little man at his side insistently.

"Sorry, Luther. Day-dreaming. Fire away."

"The last time I was in at the Middlesex Andy gave me this." He dug in the pocket of the corduroy jacket he was wearing and produced a small ticket.

"What is it?"

"A ticket to the Left Luggage office at Victoria Station."

"Go on."

"Andy said Rex had deposited a suitcase at Victoria and given the ticket to him. Now he's asked me to collect the case and keep it at my place till he gets out of hospital."

"Is it Rex's case?"

"Presumably."

"What's the hurry? Why doesn't Andy leave it till he comes out?"

"He says he's worried about it. He wants to know it's in safe, keeping."

Philip frowned. "Victoria Station is safe enough. And, anyway, if the case belongs to Rex why didn't Andy give the ticket to me? No reflection on you, old man, but after all I am his brother."

"That's just it, Philip," Harris said, blinking rapidly and running his tongue over his fat, dry lips. "Andy says there may be some private letters of his in the suitcase. He wanted to take them out before handing the case over to you."

"So he intended to give it to me eventually?"

"Well, that's what he said."

"I see." Philip switched on the ignition and made to let in the clutch. "Let's go and pick it up, then."

Harris hastily restrained him. "Hold on a tick. I'd rather not be in on this, if you don't mind."

"Why ever not? What's *in* the case? A time-bomb?"

The porky little man took off his rimless glasses and rubbed them, attempting at the same time a shaky laugh. "No, nothing like that, honest. Look here, Philip, I'll be frank with you . . . I made a mistake, I shouldn't have accepted the ticket. You see . . . well, the rozzers have already been at me two or three times about your brother and Andy, they're just itching to pin something on me just because I was a bit friendly with them both – and of course a blind man can see they were up to something fishy."

"And you just don't want to get involved, is that it?"

Harris glowed gratefully. "That's it. That's exactly what I'm trying to say."

Philip gave him a long, searching glance and shook his head. "God knows what this is all about, Luther, but you've certainly succeeded in whetting my appetite. Okay, I'll collect the suitcase myself."

Intense relief shone in Luther's weak eyes. He replaced his spectacles and said, "Thanks a million, Philip. I knew I could rely on you." He glanced over his shoulder for overtaking traffic and let himself out of the car. "I must get back to the shop."

As he closed the door he stuck his head in the window and added, in rather an obvious afterthought, "What'll you do with the case? Hand it in to the rozzers?"

Philip shrugged his shoulders. "It all depends on what's in it."

"I see. Well . . . be careful, Philip."

"Hey, are you sure it isn't a time-bomb?"

Luther smiled uncertainly. "So long, Philip," he said and walked quickly away in the direction of Admiralty Arch.

Luther's puzzling behaviour made Philip slightly uneasy as he handed in the ticket and waited at the Left Luggage office. He peered around nervously, almost expecting Hyde or Cliff Fletcher to pounce on him as the clerk, grunting with the strain, hefted the case on to the counter.

"What yer got in here, mate – yer mother-in-law?"

"How did you guess?" Philip grinned uncomfortably.

He was glad the Lancia was parked close by. By the time he reached it he was badly out of breath.

Heaving the case on to the front seat he slid behind the wheel and eyed it cautiously. At least it was not ticking. Tentatively he tried the spring catches, but was not at all surprised to find them locked.

Back at his studio he panted up the stairs with the heavy case and found that Ruth had not yet gone to her lunch. She was wearing a smart hat and coat and was just finishing a telephone call.

". . . Yes, I will, Inspector, as soon as he gets back. Goodbye."

She hung up as he closed the office door.

"Aren't you going to have any lunch today?" he asked.

"Oh, there you are," she said, her grievance temporarily forgotten. "You've just missed Inspector Hyde. You'll never guess what! They've picked up Mack-the-Knife!"

"Fletcher?"

"Yes – at least, they think it's him. They want you to go round and identify him. Isn't it exciting?"

"Yes, that really *is* good news. Where is he?"

"At Chelsea Police Station. Hyde's sending a car to pick you up." She was staring inquisitively at the suitcase. "What have you got there?"

"M'm? . . . Oh, this! It's a . . . it belonged to Rex, I believe. He left it at Victoria Station."

"Well, how did you get it?"

"Never mind now, Ruth. Run along to lunch or your salad will get cold."

She pouted indignantly but took the hint.

Directly she had gone he took a bunch of keys and tried several of them on the locks of the case, all to no avail. Reluctantly he searched for a heavy object and eventually fetched the poker from the fireplace in the living-room.

The suitcase was stoutly built and the locks took a good deal of mauling before he finally burst them open.

Philip was prepared for a surprise, but what met his gaze as he gingerly lifted the lid almost took his breath away.

At that the moment the front door-bell rang.

Chapter Ten

A tall, muscular man in a light overcoat and soft hat, with a cheerful red face and the build of a rugger player, stood at the street door.

"Mr Philip Holt, sir? Inspector Hyde asked me to collect you to drive you to Chelsea."

"Sure. Come on up. I shan't keep you waiting a moment."

Philip led the way up the stairs, saying over his shoulder, "I've got something here that's going to make the Inspector's eyes pop out of his head."

"Oh, really, sir?"

"Yes, this suitcase," Philip said as they entered the office. "Just a second while I strap it up. I had to break it open with a poker."

"It sounds intriguing, sir. What's in it?"

Philip chuckled. "You'd be amazed."

He found a strong cord and strapped it round the case. "Okay, I'm ready. Lead on, Macduff!

The policeman offered to carry the suitcase but Philip declined. They were just leaving the office when the telephone rang.

"Excuse me," Philip said as he turned back and picked up the receiver. "Philip Holt here."

"Good afternoon, sir," came a familiar voice. "Inspector Hyde speaking."

"Oh, hello, Inspector. I'm just on my way to the police station. I've got-a nice little surprise for you."

"On your way to the police station, sir? Why, has some-thing new turned up?"

"Yes, indeed it has! I'll tell you about it when we get there. Your man's just arrived."

"*My* man, Mr Holt? I'm afraid I don't quite understand."

"Inspector, you phoned a few minutes ago, didn't you, to say you'd picked up Cliff Fletcher?"

"*I* phoned you?"

"Ruth took the call. She said you wanted me to go to—"

There was a sharp click and the clatter of the telephone wall-plug as the cheerful, red-faced man – no longer quite so cheerful and now with a gun in his hand – wrenched the cable from its socket.

"All right, Smarty-pants, let's go!" he snarled, jabbing the gun sharply into Philip's ribs. "And we'll take the suitcase, since it's so interesting. Move!"

Slowly Philip bent down and grasped the case, his brain racing for a solution. Sparring for time he said, "If it's the case you want, why don't you just take it and clear out of here?"

"You've got me wrong, chum! It's you we want – you and the key."

"The key?"

"That's right – the one you failed to hand over the other evening. Only this time we're taking no chances. You've either got it on you or we'll sweat it out of you where you've hidden it. Let's go! You first, with the case."

Philip sighed and plunged one hand into his jacket pocket. "Why all the melodrama? If you want the key, here it is." He casually produced his bunch of keys in their small leather container. "Catch!" he called, and tossed them just out of the gunman's reach.

He was too slow-witted not to react in the normal instinctive manner. He swung sideways to catch the keys and in the same split second Philip hurled himself on to the arm holding the gun and twisted it backwards. The man gave a grunt of pain, and the gun clattered to the floor.

As the gunman swung a great haymaker with his free arm Philip dropped to one knee in the classic judo crouch, yanked hard on the right arm, and jerked swiftly upward as the heavy body, with considerable momentum of its own, sailed over his shoulders and landed in a clumsy sprawl two yards away.

Philip dived for the gun, but there was no need to hurry for his assailant did not move; a heavy crack on the back of the skull had knocked him unconscious.

Pocketing his keys Philip slid cautiously to the window. A powerful car – it looked like a Humber Snipe – was waiting, partly out of sight, at the corner of the street. Fletcher? It seemed probable.

Philip thought quickly. Whoever was waiting in the car would undoubtedly get worried when his stooge failed to reappear. Either he would summon up the courage to come himself and investigate, or he would drive off, leaving the gunman to his fate. Philip decided to sit it out.

In case the waiting man decided in favour of abandoning the field Philip thought a note of the car and its number-plate might come in useful. He went swiftly to the studio for his Olympus Pen F and, taking care not to show himself at the window, took a few quick shots of the car. As a precaution he also snapped the prone figure on the floor; the photographic section of Scotland Yard's rogues gallery might be glad of them. Then, seated opposite the spread-eagled body, he waited with the gun steady in his hand.

Minutes ticked by. Then eventually the unconscious figure began to stir, groaning with self-pity.

"Stay where you are!" Philip ordered. "Young Lochinvar in the car out there should be along to rescue you at any moment."

The gunman uttered an obscene oath.

"Now then, who sent you to pick me up?"

The ugly oath was repeated.

"You know, you're making me nervous," Philip said, "and this thing in my hand is liable to go off bang; I'm not nearly so accustomed to handling revolvers as you are. Now why don't you put me at my ease with a few polite answers? Who is waiting in that car down below?"

The man struggled to a sitting position, rubbed the back of his head, and began to speak "Look, Mister, I don't know anything about all this," he whined. "Honest I don't. I was just told to—"

His sentence was cut short by a revving engine and the screeching of tyres as a car rounded a sharp corner. Philip jumped to the window in time to see the car flash out of sight; a second later a police car swung round the opposite corner and slithered to a standstill.

A sudden movement behind him made him whirl round, but he was too late. His assailant had taken the chance and hurled himself out of the office and down the stairs . . . But when he tore open the street door the large frame of Sergeant Thompson barred the way, with Inspector Hyde and two police constables in close support.

"Eddie Meadows! How nice!" exclaimed the sergeant, slipping handcuffs on the man's wrists with considerable dexterity. "We've been looking for you, Eddie. You just can't keep out of trouble, can you?"

Eddie Meadows was bundled unceremoniously into the back of the police car and Hyde glanced up at Philip who now stood at the top of the stairs.

"Are you all right, Mr Holt? It was lucky I phoned you when I did, sir. I gather someone else phoned you first and you thought it was me?"

"Ruth took the call, while I was out. She said you'd be sending a car for me, so that I could identify Fletcher at Chelsea Police Station. Naturally, when that cheerful-looking creature turned up I assumed he was one of your men."

Hyde nodded. "A natural mistake, I agree. Clever of them to mention Chelsea, too. Fletcher belongs to some drinking clubs there. We've been watching his haunts for days."

"I know, I remember the cards in his wallet. They probably counted on my knowing that much."

"Quite so. Was it Fletcher waiting below?"

"I didn't get a look at the driver, but I imagine so." He took the small camera from his pocket. "But I took some snaps of the car, if that's any use. The number-plates will be clear enough."

"That was smart of you – though I don't know that it will help much; it's bound to be stolen, like the one we traced after the Windsor incident. People like Fletcher never own an honest set of plates all their lives. Anyway, what did they come for this time?"

"The key again. At first I thought it was the suitcase."

Inspector Hyde raised his eyebrows in polite inquiry. Philip smiled and led him over to the case, ripping the cord free and tossing open the lid.

As the two men stared down at the contents Hyde whistled softly. "Illuminating!" he commented. "Very illuminating . . ."

"The classic phrase is 'Coin of the Realm', I believe," Philip said cheerfully. "Only these happen to be German marks. I haven't had time to count them, but there must be thousands there."

Hyde bent down and gave the bundles of notes a quick, expert examination. Sergeant Thompson stared incredulously as he joined them. "What's the matter, Sergeant? Never seen a suitcase full of D-marke before?"

"No, as a matter of fact, sir, I haven't. Are they genuine?" Hyde nodded. "I think so."

"Someone been making you a nice Christmas present, sir?" the sergeant said, addressing Philip.

He explained in detail, while Hyde listened and Thompson counted the bundles.

"I can't help wondering," Hyde said, "if Luther Harris knew what the suitcase contained."

"I think he did," Philip replied. "But he was probably too scared to handle it. He reminds me of the chap with the hot potato in that party game."

"Then why did he agree to pick it up for Corporal Wilson in the first place?"

Philip shook his head in a puzzled fashion. "Damned if I know. Maybe he didn't want to be left holding the potato when the music stopped. How much is there, Sergeant?"

"It looks like fifty thousand marks. That's about four thousand pounds, isn't it?"

"A little bit more," said Hyde. "I think we'd better have a word with Harris, don't you, Sergeant?"

"Right, sir, I'll arrange that."

"And I wonder if I might ask you to drop in to see me at the Yard, Mr Holt? Say some time around four o'clock this afternoon?"

"I'll be there, Inspector."

"Thank you so much. Goodbye for now."

Hyde's office at Scotland Yard was neat and impersonal, an accurate reflection of its occupier. Files lay stacked tidily on the large
mahogany desk, a rack of carefully sharpened pencils stood like
space-rockets on guard near the telephone, with a scribbling block
of virginal white close at hand. The only ornament of any kind
was a photograph of Hyde's family in a green leather frame.

The aroma of the Inspector's strong pipe tobacco hung in the
air; Luther Harris, who sat facing Hyde and fidgeting nervously,
had evidently been under cross-examination for some time.

He looked relieved at the interruption as Philip was shown
into the room, but Hyde merely waved his visitor to a vacant
chair and continued with quiet authority. "I'm not convinced that
you're telling me the whole truth, Mr Harris. Let's start again
from the beginning."

"I've told you how it was, Inspector, honest I have! I'm not
mixed up in this affair at all. Just because I knew Rex and Andy,
that doesn't mean a thing! I run a perfectly respectable music
shop in Tottenham Court Road – the Top Twenty's my bread and
butter and—"

"When did Corporal Wilson give you the ticket?" Hyde asked
coldly.

"Er . . . The ticket? . . . Well, it was when I visited him at the
Middlesex. He asked me to go down to Victoria and pick up this
case of Rex's. I was to bring it to him at the hospital, so that he could
take some things of his out. Perhaps that was a little joke of his, I
mean, maybe he meant all that German lolly, I don't know. Anyway,
afterwards he was going to hand the case over to Mr Holt here."

"And you agreed to collect the case?"

"Yes, I did. Only—"

"Why did you change your mind and pass the buck to
Mr Holt?"

"Well, I . . . I sort of had second thoughts about the matter, if
you get me?"

"No, I don't get you, Mr Harris."

Luther stuttered in confusion and shot Philip a beseeching look, which the latter ignored.

Then Hyde struck home. "You knew what was in the case, didn't you?"

"No! I keep telling you, I'd no idea what was in it! I still can't believe there were fifty thousand marks in it. Where on earth did Rex or Andy get hold of money like that?"

The Inspector made no answer but started giving his pipe a lengthy rebore. Eventually he turned again to the obviously uncomfortable man in front of him. "How often did Wilson and Rex Holt visit your shop?"

"They dropped in quite often when they had a spot of leave."

"Did they ever meet anyone there? By appointment, I mean."

Luther considered for a moment. "No, I don't think so."

"Are you sure?"

"Well . . . there was one occasion . . .

"Go on, Mr Harris."

"Several months ago a woman came into the shop and asked for a particular record. It was in big demand and I'd only one left, and it so happened that Rex was listening to it in one of the cubicles. I told him the woman wanted to listen to the record and instead of handing it over he worked that old charm of his and invited her into the cubicle. I was a bit peeved at the time, because neither Rex nor Andy ever actually bought anything; they just came for a free concert. But things worked out all right in the end, the woman bought the record herself."

"Did you get the impression Rex had met her before?" Philip asked.

"I'm not sure. Perhaps he hadn't met her – but I got the feeling maybe he'd been expecting her."

"What was she like, this woman? Can you describe her?"

"Yes. She was smart, sure of herself – a bit hoity-toity, if you get me. Be around forty, maybe a bit older. She had a check suit, with a diamond and ruby brooch on the lapel."

"Was the brooch shaped like a basket of flowers?" Philip asked sharply.

"Yes. As a matter of fact it was. How did you guess?"

The Inspector took the pipe out of his mouth and leant forward. "Does that ring a bell then, Mr Holt?"

"I'm not sure – but it sounds remarkably like Mrs Clare Seldon to me."

Hyde nodded, and when he addressed Luther Harris his manner was less frosty than before. "This is an interesting lead you've given us." Luther beamed and Hyde added, "Has this woman ever been back to Pop's Corner?"

"No, never."

"And you've never seen her since?"

"I'm afraid not, Inspector."

"I see."

There was a tap on the door and Sergeant Thompson entered, carrying a sheaf of photographs. Hyde motioned to him to wait for a moment and turned to Luther Harris again. "Was Corporal Wilson in the shop when this woman met Rex?"

The answer came pat. "No, he wasn't. If I remember rightly he turned up about half an hour later."

Hyde gave him a bleak look, then stretched out a hand for the photographs. He glanced at them, nodded, and passed them across to Philip. "I'd like you to take a look at these. Interpol dug them out and sent them over from the Continent this morning."

Philip took one look at the prints and stiffened. "Fletcher !" he said emphatically. "Or, as Ruth would say, Mack-the-Knife."

"You're quite sure?"

"Absolutely certain."

"Good. Maybe this case is beginning to make sense at last. Take a look, Mr Harris. Have you ever met this gentleman?"

It was perhaps fortunate for Luther Harris that his thick spectacles prevented too close an observation of his eyes, but he could not disguise the faint trembling of his fingers as he replaced the photographs on the desk.

"No, I'm afraid not, Inspector."

"Oh. You disappoint me. Are you quite sure?"

"Yes, quite sure."

"I see. Sergeant, has our friend Eddie Meadows been given the opportunity to study these prints?"

"Yes, sir. He claims he doesn't know him from Adam. He's lying, though."

"And he's still sticking to the same little fairy-story as to why he called on Mr Holt this afternoon?"

"He is, sir. Says he knows nothing about it except that he was told to pick up Mr Holt and bring him down to the waiting car."

Inspector Hyde studied his pipe. "H'm . . . It's possible, I suppose."

"I think so, sir," Thompson agreed. "Eddie Meadows hasn't got the brains of a louse, I think he'd just be carrying out orders. There was fifty pounds on him, which sounds like a typical Fletcher payment for a job like that."

Hyde grunted irritably. "All we've caught is a sardine, while the killer-whale is still swimming around. What the devil's the matter with our underground contacts these days? You'd better spread it abroad, Sergeant, that we'll pay an extra high price for any useful tip on Fletcher's whereabouts."

"I'll do that, sir."

"It's ridiculous – we know what he looks like, we've got a first-class set of prints on that knife he threw at. Mr Holt, we've got a case that would really stand up in court, but we haven't got the man himself!"

"Who *is* he; then, Inspector?" Philip asked. "Up to now I hadn't thought of him as being more than a slick thug with a knife, but now that you talk of Interpol . . ."

"His real name is Sandman – Peter Sandman – but he works under several aliases. Cliff Fletcher happens to be one of them. The West German police think he organised that big Hamburg bank robbery about eighteen months ago. You remember the case – the Head Cashier was an Englishman named Weston working on a twelve-month exchange scheme; he was murdered as he came out of his office one night. The murder weapon was a switch-blade knife."

Philip shook his head. "I don't remember the case. Where did you say this happened?"

Inspector Hyde tapped out his pipe and said with quiet finality, "Hamburg, sir. Where your brother and Corporal Wilson were stationed at the time, I think."

Philip grew tense. "Wait a moment – do you mean . . ."

"Inspector, I've got to get back to the shop," Luther said hastily. "Are you finished with me?"

"Yes, for the time being, Mr Harris. But you won't be leaving Town for the next few days, will you? I shouldn't advise it."

When Philip left Scotland Yard some twenty minutes later he found, to his surprise, that Luther Harris was loitering near the Lancia.

"Hello, Luther, I thought you were in a hurry to get back to the shop."

"That was just an excuse to get clear of that place. All those rozzers give me the creeps. That's the third time they've grilled me since Rex's death. I'm getting sick and tired of it, I can tell you."

"I can imagine," said Philip dryly. "Want me to drop you off anywhere?"

"That's very nice of you."

"So they've questioned you twice before, have they, Luther?" Philip said as they drove up Whitehall.

"Yes. The day after Rex died they came to the shop and poked their noses around. God knows what they hoped to find – the murder weapon hidden in a trombone or something. Then that suspicious bastard, Hyde, dropped in again the morning after I'd been to the hospital to see Andy."

"Sounds like pure routine to me, Luther. They'll have had to check up on all sorts of people, anyone connected with Rex who might give them a lead on the case."

"I wish to heaven they'd turn the heat off me, that's all."

"Yes, but it's only natural that Hyde wanted to talk to you about the suitcase, Luther. When I saw all that money I had to mention how the case came into my possession."

"Of course. I'm not blaming you, old sport. What peeves me about the coppers is that they have one-track minds. Anyone would think my shop was the only place where Rex and Andy ever went!"

"Where else did they go, Luther?"

"There were dozens of other places. There was that coffee bar near Knightsbridge Barracks, for instance. They spent a lot of time there, I know."

"I don't think I know it. What's it called?"

"The *El* something or other. Fancy Spanish name, I think . . . Wait a tick, the El Barbecue – that's it!"

"And they went there often?"

"Yes, frequently."

"Well, was there anything odd about that?"

"No, but   "

"I dare say there was some snappy waitress there who'd taken Rex's eye."

"No, there's no waitresses. It's run by a fat feller named Oscar and his wife. There was one waiter, chap named Joseph, Swiss I believe."

"You've been there yourself, then?"

"Once or twice, when the boys got me along for a night out. Personally, I should have thought it was worth the coppers' while to give that little joint the once-over, instead of plaguing the life out of me all the time."

"The El Barbecue, eh? M'm . . . Is it all right if I drop you off near the Circus?"

"Suits me fine. Thanks for the lift. Be seeing you, old sport."

As Philip swung left out of Cambridge Circus and down Shaftesbury Avenue he debated the alternatives. It was perfectly clear what Luther wanted him to do. If he had really intended the police to take an interest in the El Barbecue coffee bar Luther would have given the tip straight to Inspector Hyde. Philip wondered whether Luther was trying to cover up for something that the irresponsible Rex might have done. The two had been good friends; it was just possible that he still felt some bond of obligation towards the dead man.

Whatever the reason, Philip could see no grounds for not acting on the heavy hint. If he kept his eyes and ears open it could surely do no harm, and it might lead to something. He had reached the stage where he felt that any lead was better than none.

The El Barbecue was a café that showed signs of wear and tear from the heavy boots of its principal clientele – soldiers from Knightsbridge Barracks.

It was relatively empty and Philip had his choice of the red-upholstered stools at the coffee bar or any one of several formica-topped tables near by. There was no sign of a Swiss waiter. A big, tough looking man with a shiny bald head sat behind the bar, picking his teeth and reading an evening paper. He continued to read it when a distant shout of "Oscar!" reached his ears, acknowledging the call with an unintelligible growl.

Philip sat on a stool and ordered coffee, and eventually the bald-headed man served him with complete absence of grace.

Presently a tired, irritable-looking woman in a soiled apron came through a swing-door from the kitchens and slammed huge, freshly cut sandwiches on to the counter. She threw a disinterested look at the few customers and began a noisy attack on a pile of washing-up. The bald-headed man offered no help, but concentrated on his toothpick and his reading.

Philip coughed. "Er – excuse me . . . er – Oscar, isn't it?"

"Yes," the fat man replied laconically without looking up.

"My name's Philip Holt. I wonder if you can help me?"

For a fraction of a second the toothpick ceased its gouging, and the rattle of the washing-up was stilled. Then Oscar and the woman continued with their preoccupations.

"Yes?"

"I'm making certain inquiries about my brother Rex. He was a soldier and he used to come here quite a lot when he was on leave."

"Well?"

"I was wondering if you remember him? He was tall, very fair, good looking.

"We get a lot of soldiers here, Mister."

"Yes, I realise that. But you may have seen my brother's name and picture in the papers lately. He committed suicide."

Again there was a tiny pause in the rattle of cups.

Oscar made no move. "Did he come here alone?"

"No, he was generally tagging along with a corporal, a chap named Andy Wilson – short, stocky, thinning yellow hair. Both of them were jazz fans."

Oscar shrugged his mountainous shoulders. "Do you remember anyone like that, Joyce?" he called without looking round.

Despite her chores at the sink Joyce appeared to have missed none of the conversation. "No, can't say I do. We get hundreds of army lads here, you know."

Philip persisted. "Well, how about your waiter? Joseph, is it? Swiss, I believe Rex said he was. Perhaps I could have a word with him?"

"Joseph? He doesn't work here any more."

"Oh."

It looked like a dead end. Oscar and the tired woman were not over anxious to be helpful. And yet Luther had obviously wanted to steer Philip to this spot. Then he recalled the second of taut silence which the name Holt had prompted and was encouraged to try again.

"Do you happen to know where Joseph is working now?" he asked.

"Some pub down the Brompton Road," Oscar said off-handedly. "But if you stick around maybe you'll see him. He generally drops in for a cup of coffee around this time."

"Thanks. I'll do that. How will I recognise him?"

"Take a pew over there," Oscar said, nodding towards a corner table at the other end of the café. "I'll let you know if he turns up."

Philip expressed his thanks and ordered another cup of coffee. Oscar curtly passed the order on to the woman and after a moment disappeared through the swing-door.

As Philip took the coffee and walked towards the corner table a faint impression of sound registered at the back of his consciousness; but he had taken his place at the table and stirred three lumps of sugar into his coffee before that faint impression swam to the surface to become identified. It had been the click and tinkle of a telephone receiver being lifted.

He took out a cigarette but did not light it, and, pretending to be absorbed in a discarded newspaper which lay on the table, he listened intently. In less than a minute the sound was repeated – obviously the telephone receiver had been replaced – and soon afterwards Oscar came through the swing-door. He murmured something to the woman at the sink and, without glancing across at Philip, resumed his labours with toothpick and evening newspaper.

Philip watched the customers come in and out. They were mostly soldiers. A few were greeted by Oscar or Joyce with a perfunctory show of friendliness, but for the most part the dull weight of surly, sub-standard service hung like a pall over the scene. The minutes ticked by.

Then Philip suddenly realised that Oscar had quietly faded out of the picture. There was no sign of Joyce either. An entirely fresh face, that of a pert young girl wearing a chequered apron, appeared from behind the espresso coffee machine as she polished it and admired her reflection in its shining surface.

Philip rose and strolled over to her. "Where's everyone got to?" he asked.

"I don't know what you mean," she said indifferently.
"Where's Oscar?"

"Back there, in the kitchen, having supper."

"I see."

He turned back to his table, then halted sharply. A woman had taken the vacant seat opposite his own, and there was something vaguely familiar about the outline of her back. She did not look up as he walked past her and slid into his seat

Curiously, he looked at her and said quietly, "You wouldn't by any chance be Joseph, would you?"

Chapter Eleven

Clare Seldon gave a short, impatient toss of her head. She looked sharply out of place in the seedy café.

With perfect composure she lit a cigarette, and took her time about crushing the spent match in the ashtray. "Still playing the amateur sleuth, Mr Holt?"

"That's right."

"You're a tryer, aren't you? When are you going to give up?"

Philip ignored the question and retorted, "How did you know I was here? Did Oscar tip you off, or was it Luther Harris? Odd company you keep, Mrs Seldon. How's our mutual friend Cliff Fletcher these days? Getting in plenty of practice with his flick-knife, is he?"

"You're lucky to be alive, Mr Holt. Cliff Fletcher doesn't often bungle things. Had you been a more sensible man you'd have retired from the scene long ago."

Philip sighed. "I fear this is the moment for that heroic little speech I've been trying to avoid. I'm not going to give up or retire from the scene until I've found out who murdered my brother, and brought that murderer to justice. Would you please relay that statement to the gentlemen with whom you are so curiously associated?"

Clare Seldon appeared to weigh his words carefully, then nodded. "That's more or less what I expected. Stupidity and stubbornness so often go hand in hand. Very well, Mr Holt. I have a proposition to make to you. It's very simple: you give me something I want and I'll supply you with certain facts which appear to obsess you."

"Such as?"

"Why your brother went to Maidenhead. Why he was studying that book of Belloc's verse. What Thomas Quayle had to do with the affair. And quite a lot else, but that will do for a start."

"If you know so much I wonder what there is to prevent me from hitting you over the head with this ashtray and carting you off to the nearest police station."

Mrs Seldon gave him a pitying smile. "Oscar, perhaps? Oscar might prevent you."

"I see."

"Good. Then let's be sensible. Does my proposition interest you?"

"What's my side of the deal?"

"You simply have to hand over the parcel to me."

"What parcel?"

"The one that was sent from Germany to your brother, care of your flat."

"Nothing like that has turned up."

"Are you sure?"

"Yes, unless it came with this evening's post"

"Very well. All you have to do is sit tight till it arrives. Run shouting to the police and you'll get precisely nothing out of me; play ball, and you'll get to know the real truth about your brother."

Philip considered the proposition carefully. At length he said, "How do I find you?"

"You don't. I haven't the least intention of inviting Inspector Hyde or any other policeman on to my doorstep." She dipped into her smart leather handbag and produced a slip of paper on which a telephone number was typed. "When the parcel arrives you just ring this number and you'll be told what to do. If you attempt anything clever, such as trying to trace this number or mentioning the meeting to Hyde, our deal is cancelled. Is that quite clear?"

"Yes, that's quite clear. You know, Mrs Seldon, what amazes me is how neat and matter-of-fact you make it all sound. Anyone sitting a few tables away would never dream that we'd just completed a sordid little contract connected with murder."

She ground her cigarette into the ashtray arid stood up. "I'm happy to hear you use that word 'contract', Mr Holt. We're in business, and it's not the kiddies' woolly toy department. I shall expect to hear from you."

She swept out of the coffee bar, looking neither to right nor left. And as usual the faint scent of a good quality perfume hung in the air.

Two days passed, while Philip watched the post with increasing nervousness and irritability. He was honest enough to realise that it was not only the non-arrival of the parcel which was troubling him; his conscience had begun to chafe. He had promised to co-operate with Inspector Hyde, to make all his moves in the open, and to try nothing spectacular on the side; yet here he was, doing exactly the opposite. He argued with himself that if the police should show signs of knowing that something was afoot Clare Seldon might take fright and disappear before she had fulfilled her side of the bargain. For this reason he did not contact Luther Harris either, although there were some hard questions he would have liked to have put to that evasive gentleman.

But his conscience still chafed and he grew steadily more irritable. As Ruth was nearest to hand she bore the brunt of his bad temper. Matters came to a head late in the afternoon of the second day of waiting, as outside in the streets a high tension rainstorm marked the end of a long, hot spell of weather that had-also not helped his nerves.

Ostensibly they quarrelled about the post.

"Not so long ago you at least acknowledged that I was 'just a very efficient secretary'," she burst out, two bright pink spots of anger glowing on her smooth cheeks. "Now you don't even let me open the post!"

"I'm sorry. I know I'm on edge these days. I'm expecting something and it just hasn't turned up, that's all. I can't understand the delay."

"It still doesn't transform me into an entirely useless appendage!"

"I'm very sorry if you feel you must act the slighted young lady, but I can't afford to run the risk of having this . . . this thing I'm expecting misplaced or lost."

"You're the one who's always misplacing things in this studio, not me! There's a far bigger chance of things getting lost if you—"

"Ruth, do stop nagging ! The way you women go on and on . . ."

"I'm only trying to help," she wailed, a suspicion of tears in her eyes.

"Like you did with that bungled telephone call from Eddie Meadows?" he snapped.

He knew he had been unfair, and instantly, as her tears came, he regretted the harshness of his words.

Slowly she replaced the cover on her typewriter, set a stack of prints in neat order, and dabbed at her eyes. Taking her hat and raincoat from the coat-hanger she murmured, "Perhaps it's time you started looking for a new secretary, Mr Holt."

Her high heels clattered down the stairs and she let herself out into the street. The front door slammed and a blast of cold damp air flooded the office.

"That's all I needed!" Philip sank into a chair and stared listlessly at a vast pile of work which was badly in arrears. Five minutes later the door-bell rang.

Douglas Talbot stood on the threshold, shaking the rain off his umbrella, and booming as though he were on the bridge of a mighty warship.

"I do hope I'm not disturbing you, Holt. I thought you ought to have this." He thrust a small parcel into Philip's hands. "It came from Germany and it's addressed to your brother. God knows why they sent it to the hotel."

Philip took the parcel eagerly. It was rectangular and bore a Hamburg postmark, but the date was indecipherable. "That's very kind of you, Mr Talbot. I hope you haven't come all the way from Maidenhead just to deliver this?"

"Oh no! I had to see a man about some student staff from the catering school in Vincent Square. It occurred to Mrs Curtis that as I was in the area I might as well drop it in. It's really Mrs Curtis you have to thank, not me."

"Well, I'm very glad to have it."

Out of sheer politeness, though he was most anxious to open the parcel, Philip added, "Won't you come in out of the rain and have a drink?"

Talbot looked at his watch. "I think I've just got time for a quick one. Thank you."

Philip led the way up the stairs and through the office into his flat.

Talbot sat down in a wing-backed chair and stretched his long legs to-their full length; Philip had to walk round them in order to reach the drinks cabinet. He placed a bottle of whisky, two glasses, and a soda siphon on a small table between them and began a search for cigarettes.

"How's Mrs Curtis?" Philip asked.

By the time he had found the cigarettes Talbot had helped himself to a liberal portion of Dimple Haig.

"Oh, much the same, you know. She's a nervy little woman."

"She's had rather a lot to make her nervy, wouldn't you say? What with my brother's suicide, that near miss in the street at Windsor, and then the frightful murder of her brother, it's rather a lot for anyone to have to bear inside a few weeks."

"Yes, I suppose the poor woman has had rather a rough time," he agreed. "She's taking it pretty well on the whole." Philip raised his glass. "Your health!"

"Cheers !" Talbot took a large gulp from his glass.

"Have there been any developments in the Quayle case?" Philip went on.

"I wouldn't know. The police don't take me into their confidence, I assure you. They've been down to the hotel several times, badgering Vanessa and me with a variety of questions, but they don't seem to be getting anywhere. That fellow Hyde doesn't cut much ice, if you ask me. Incidentally, I understand you told him that Quayle came here and asked for that key?"

"Yes, he did."

"What a strange thing to do. Thomas knew perfectly well it belonged to his sister. It's the key to her private suite, you know."

"Yes, so the Inspector told me."

"It's my opinion that old Thomas was up to something – bit of a dark horse."

"Did you know him well?"

"Thomas? No, not really. To be frank with you, all that affectation with the wretched little dog, and his peculiar taste in clothes . . . Well, not to put too fine a point on it, he wasn't really my cup of tea . . . But he was up to something, you can bet your life on that." He drained his whisky glass. "People don't get themselves knifed in the back for nothing."

"No, I don't suppose they do," said Philip wryly.

Talbot glanced at his watch and stood up. "I must be on my way. Thanks for the drink."

"A pleasure. I'm most grateful to you for bringing the parcel."

"No trouble at all."

Philip could hardly wait till he had closed the street door on the pompous hotel manager. Taking the stairs two at a time he darted back to the living-room and slit the parcel open with a pocket knife.

The brown wrapping paper fell away to reveal corrugated cardboard fastened by a rubber band. He ripped the content free.

It was a small, slim book; a familiar book. *Sonnets and Verse* by Hilaire Belloc – the same edition as the one Rex had studied and Andy had stolen, but not the same copy. This one had a brief notation inside the fly-leaf, in a spidery foreign hand. It read:

Hier ist das Buch das Du brauchst. LINDERHOF.

Philip puzzled over the translation for a moment, not sure what the final word meant. "Here is the book that you . . . want? Need? Forgot? Bought?" Several suggestions made sense. He studied the handwriting, then hurried to the dark-room to consult the rough proofs of the hotel guest register. He found Dr Linderhof's entry; the handwriting tallied.

He pondered over the message a while longer, and made a

126

detailed examination of the book, without discovering anything new. Then finally he took out the slip of paper Clare Seldon had given him and dialled the number.

"Yes?" answered a coarse male voice.

"Can I speak to Mrs Clare Seldon, please?"

"Who wants her?"

"Philip Holt."

There was a short silence. Then, "Hold the line."

He had to wait two minutes before he heard her voice. "Yes, Mr Holt? This is Clare Seldon."

"I thought I'd let you know the parcel's just arrived."

"I see. Well, now it's up to you."

"What do you mean?"

"Do you want to meet me, Mr Holt?"

"If I hadn't wanted to meet you I wouldn't be phoning, would I?"

"You might . . . if you'd been in touch with the police."

"I haven't, Mrs Seldon. I give you my word on that."

She appeared to hesitate. "You'd be a fool to try and trick me."

"I know, I know – you're in business and it's not the kiddies' woolly toy department. When and where do we meet? The Savoy Grill at eight-thirty?"

The voice that answered was again crisp and pragmatic. "Do you know Blackgate Common?"

"Yes."

"Then listen carefully. On the north side of the common there's an old horse-trough. About thirty yards away a lane leads down to a farm – Blackgate Farm, it's called. I'll park my car about halfway down this lane. It's fifty yards or so off the main road."

"Very well."

"Bring the parcel. I'll see you there in about two hours time. All right?"

"I'll be there."

"Good. Don't be late."

The phone clicked dead.

Philip replaced the receiver. This was a venture which required careful thought.

He realised that by the time he reached Blackgate Common it would be dark, and it was a lonely spot. He was quite capable of coping with the cool Mrs Seldon, but what if she had Cliff Fletcher, or someone else with a knife, hidden in the back of her car? He felt tempted to get in touch with Hyde and arrange for discreet protection, then brushed the thought from his mind. His pride demanded that he go through with this incident on his own, and common sense told him that Clare Seldon would not remain long at their trysting place if she smelt so much as a whiff of police interference.

There was still no harm in taking a few precautions, however. He unlocked the wall-safe in his bedroom and took out the revolver which had once belonged to Eddie Meadows. He had failed to hand it in to the police at the time, and in the excitement caused by Eddie Meadows' arrest and the suitcases full of German money the gun had somehow escaped their attention.

He put the revolver into his briefcase with the book of poems and a small but powerful torch. Then he selected a large-scale map of South London which included the area around Blackgate Common and pored over it for several minutes.

He was perfectly willing to meet Clare Seldon at the spot suggested, but saw no reason to stick to the approach route which she had dictated. He decided to park his car a quarter of a mile away at least, leave the book in the glove compartment, and walk quietly across the common, gun and torch in hand. He would not announce his presence until he was certain that the woman was alone and keeping to the rules. She would see that he was armed, and when he was satisfied that the back seat or the boot of her car did not house a third person he would compel her to drive him back to his own car, and there trade Linderhof's book for the information he wanted.

It was not a foolproof plan, but it was the best he could think of in the short time at his disposal. He stuffed the map into his briefcase, slipped on his raincoat, and started down the stairs.

As he did so a key was fitted into the street door and Ruth let herself in. She looked petite and helpless and very appealing in a white mackintosh and a white elfin cap. They stood staring at one another for a long moment, then she gave a diffident smile.

"I'm sorry for the histrionics this afternoon," she said. "Am I still on the pay-roll or have you got yourself a new secretary in the meantime?"

Philip felt a wave of relief surge over him. "It's my job to do some apologising, not yours. Come in out of the rain, Ruth," he said gently, and the tension was over. "What are you doing coming back at this time of the night, anyway?"

"Well, if you must know, I thought I'd do a little overtime. There's that conceited M.P.'s portrait that needs retouching, and the toothpaste ad. we promised by tomorrow, and I don't know how many other jobs that we're behind schedule on."

"I don't know how I'd manage without you, Ruth," Philip confessed, running up the stairs again and opening the door for her.

She brushed past him with a slight but perceptible trembling and peeled off her wet coat. "That's just what I keep telling you," she said rather shakily. "I say, are you off somewhere?"

"I'm afraid so. If I'm not back afore sundown, round up a posse and head 'em off at the gulch!"

"Head who off?"

Philip laughed, but there was evidently something about his tone that belied his attempt at light-heartedness. Ruth gave him a searching look. She knew him well.

"Is something wrong, Philip?"

"Maybe. Listen, you read German, don't you?"

"A little."

He took out the Belloc poems and showed her Linderhof's inscription. "What do you make of this?"

"*Here is the book . . . the book which you need,*" she translated carefully. "Isn't that the same book that Rex was supposed to be . . . Hey! what have you got there?" she demanded swiftly as Philip tried to snap the briefcase shut. "I didn't know you owned a gun!"

129

"I don't. It belonged to Eddie Meadows. I 'forgot' to give it to the Inspector."

"Philip, what *is* all this?" Ruth looked worried.

He ran down the stairs, calling over his shoulder, "Tell you all about it when I get back, poppet. And if I don't get back, please remember that posse!"

"Poppet!" she said to herself as the door slammed. "Well, I suppose I can notch that one up as a promotion – it's certainly an advance on 'just a very efficient secretary'."

The drive to Blackgate Common through wet, crowded streets was tedious and exasperating. Except on occasional stretches of straight road the throaty power of the Lancia was of little use to him. He concentrated on driving, ignoring the blandishments of other cars on the road which would normally have set him day-dreaming about future purchases.

Well over an hour had passed by the time he reached the fringes of Blackgate Common. He pulled into the side of the road and studied his map carefully.

Satisfied, he ignored the road which he had been ordered to take and instead swung south, looking out for a third-class road that, according to the map, transversed the common from north to south. After five minutes he spotted it. It was little more than a muddy cart-track.

He turned into it, changed down, and using only sidelights crawled slowly through the thick woods until he reached a clearing where chopped wood lay stacked in uneven piles. He switched off the ignition and sidelights, lowered the window, and sat absolutely still for five minutes.

The rain had mercifully ceased. There was nothing to be heard except the dripping of water from sodden leaves and the occasional hoot of an owl. There was no moon, but a weak radiance filtered through the cloud so that once his eyes had grown accustomed to the darkness he was able to see for some ten to twenty yards.

He was nearly twenty minutes late. There was probably no

harm in this; Clare Seldon would wait, and it might even be to his advantage to put her a little on edge.

The Belloc poems were safely locked in the glove compartment, the gun in his raincoat pocket. Gripping his unlit torch, he stepped quietly out of the car . . .

It was easy going so long as he kept to the cart-track where sodden leaves, mingled with the soft mud churned up by a forester's cart or tractor, allowed him to tread silently.

Five minutes later, at a second clearing, he sensed that he must be near the road that spanned the northern boundaries of the common and ducked swiftly into the woods to gain cover for his final approach.

Here his discomfort began. Thick undergrowth, sharp brambles, and slimy fern impeded his progress, and more than once a supple branch swung back and whipped his face with a stinging blow. Cold raindrops from the disturbed branches splashed down the back of his neck, and unseen night-beasts twittered in panic when some dry twigs cracked unnervingly beneath his foot. Once more an owl hooted, then all was silent again.

The snapped deadwood increased his caution. Step by step, testing the undergrowth before him, he moved with infinite stealth until a shifting in the quality of the light told him he had reached the road.

He paused, his ears strained for the slightest sound, his eyes searching for the road. Then from the distance came the unmistakable sound of a car changing gear uphill.

He darted across the road in four large strides, and here in the deeper shadow he stole along the ditch until the faint outline of a horse-trough came into view.

As he reached it a frightful screech split the night and he dropped like a stone as a bird flashed from a bush squawking frantically. He went on, his heart thudding, and came to a lonely signpost swaying like a ghostly gibbet in the wind. He could just make out the words BLACKGATE FARM on the creaking metal signplate, and then he saw the lane, branching off at right-angles, where Mrs Seldon had arranged to park her car.

He took the gun firmly in his right hand, the torch in his left, and crept on in the shadow of a line of dripping rhododendron bushes.

The dim shape of a parked car appeared at last, and it was something of an anti-climax to discover that it was empty. Shielding the torch till it was no more than a pencilled beam of light, he flicked it over the car's interior and then, taking his courage in both hands, opened the boot.

That, too, was empty, except for a tool-kit and a pair of women's overshoes of the transparent plastic type worn over smart high heels. He felt little doubt that the overshoes belonged to Clare Seldon, and on examining the ground near the driver's door he was just able to detect the imprints of high-heeled shoes leading away from the car. His hand tightened on the gun and he followed.

He had been right about the high heels.

They protruded from a bush about twenty yards away, and still managed to look smart on the silk-stockinged legs of the dead woman. She lay, with a knife in her back, under a discreet covering of sodden undergrowth.

Chapter Twelve

Philip did not touch Clare Seldon's body.

He shone his torch on the knife; which bore a strong similarity to the weapon which had killed Quayle and to the one that had finished up inside a box-file in his studio. He searched for signs of male footprints, then quickly switched off the torch as the sound of an approaching car met his ears.

Headlights wheeled and flickered in the woods to his left and he waited for the car to roar past on the main road, but instead it swung off into the lane, picking out Clare Seldon's parked car in a flood of light

Philip was stunned by the sight of uniformed policemen silhouetted in the headlights as doors slammed and boots pounded on the road. He recognised Inspector Hyde's quiet but penetrating voice giving calm orders and realised that his own position was far from favourable. He walked slowly towards the police car and managed to discern Hyde's outline among the medley of figures.

Hyde caught sight of him. "Mr Holt! Are you all right?"

"Yes, I'm fine. How on earth did you know—"

"Tell me quickly what happened!"

"I haven't got it quite clear myself yet. You'll find Clare Seldon in the bushes a few yards down the lane there, with a knife in her back. This time," he added grimly, "I haven't touched the knife."

Hyde issued swift instructions to Sergeant Thompson, who was among the small squad accompanying him. "I'll be there in a moment!" he called out as Thompson hurried down the lane.

"Inspector, how on earth did you happen to turn up here?" Philip asked.

"We received an anonymous telephone call from a woman. She told us you were going to Blackgate Common and she thought someone had planned to murder you. I'll save the lecture on our 'mutual co-operation treaty' till later, Mr Holt," he went on crisply. "Perhaps you can tell me who the woman was?"

"I've no idea. Did you speak to her personally?"

"Yes, the call was put through to me."

"And you didn't recognise the voice?"

"I've an idea the voice was disguised."

"No one knew I had an appointment with Clare Seldon. The only person who knew I was going out was my secretary, and she didn't know *where*."

"Well, we'll discuss it later. I have disagreeable work to do."

With shoulders hunched and hands thrust deep into his trench-coat pockets Hyde marched down the lane to join the team who, by the light of powerful sodium lamps, were engaged in roping off and examining the scene of the crime.

Half an hour later Philip was once again at the wheel of the Lancia, heading towards London. Rain had again set in, and the Inspector had decided that there was little point in Philip hanging around in the inhospitable night while the tedious investigations of the homicide squad continued. They had arranged to meet at Scotland Yard early the following morning.

The rush-hour traffic was long over and he made good time on the return journey. He looked forward to a stiff drink at his flat and then, if by any chance she was still working, he would take Ruth out for a good meal. He was not yet prepared to analyse his feelings about the girl, but he had to admit to a sense of chilly desolation during the interval after his bad temper had prompted her to walk out.

As he entered the office and switched on the lights a gasp of rage and shock escaped from him.

The room looked as though a herd of wild horses had ridden through it. Drawers lay open with their contents strewn about the floor, files were scattered in wild profusion, boxes of film mingled with the personal knick-knacks on his desk. The cushion of Ruth's chair had been ripped open.

Automatically he bent down to pick up her overturned chair, and as he did so his eye was caught by a tiny silver horseshoe shining on the carpet. Then he recognised the broken charm bracelet lying a few feet away and a cold, sinking sensation struck his heart. He looked up at the coat-rack and his worst suspicions were confirmed: Ruth's white rain-coat and little elfin cap were still in place. She had evidently not left the office of her own free will . . .

"Good evening, Mr Holt," said a familiar voice behind him.

Philip spun round and found himself looking down the barrel of a revolver held steadily in the hand of Cliff Fletcher. "How the devil did you get in here, Fletcher?" he shouted.

"I could tell you I picked the lock like last time, but it actually wasn't necessary. We rang the bell and that neat little skirt of yours obligingly let us in."

"Where is she?"

Fletcher looked at the coat-rack in feigned surprise. "She seems to have gone out, doesn't she? And without her coat too, on a nasty night like this."

'What the devil have you done with her? Isn't one body per day enough for you?"

"What are you talking about, Mr Holt?"

"You know damn well I'm talking about Clare Seldon!"

"Oh dear, has something happened to Clare? I am sorry."

"I suppose you're going to tell me you had nothing to do with it.

"I've been up in Town all evening having a few drinks with some friends of mine in Chelsea. You're welcome to check on that any time you like."

"I wouldn't waste my time," Philip snapped. "You'll have paid well enough to have your alibi confirmed. Though I don't recall mentioning the fact that it happened tonight, and it must be a damn funny part of Chelsea you've been drinking in, to get the mud of Blackgate Common on your shoes."

Fletcher frowned and glanced down. There were traces of mud around the edges of his soles. "Careless of me, I must admit . . .

135

Stay just where you are!" he barked as Philip, tempted by the momentary distraction, braced himself to lunge forward. "Now then, let's get down to business. Hand over the key and I'll guarantee to have your nice little bit of skirt back here inside fifteen minutes."

"Alive or dead?"

"When I last saw her she was alive and kicking, – kicking a damn sight too much, as a matter of fact. If you behave sensibly she won't get hurt."

"Am I supposed to believe that?"

"I'm on the level about this. The girl doesn't interest us. Hand me the key and you get the girl back undamaged."

"You'll get the key when I know she's all right; and when I know she's free." '

Fletcher sighed, considered for a moment, then crossed to the telephone. The gun remained trained on Philip as he lifted the receiver and placed it on the desk. He dialled with his left hand.

"This is Cliff . . . Yeah, he's here. Release the girl . . . Don't argue, do as I say! Tell her to phone Holt from a call-box so she can prove she's free. Make it snappy!" He replaced the receiver and stretched out his hand. "Give!"

"Not until Ruth rings me."

Fletcher swore, and then settled himself comfortably with one leg swinging nonchalantly over the corner of the desk. "Okay, we'll sit this one out together."

Nearly ten minutes, which seemed like an eternity, dragged by before the ringing of the telephone jarred the silence.

Philip moved but Fletcher snapped at him. "Oh no, you don't! It could just be Hyde or some other pal of yours." He picked up the receiver himself. "Yes?" Then he nodded. "It's her."

Philip grabbed the receiver. "Ruth? . . . Are you all right? . . . Is there anyone with you? . . . Are you sure? . . . Where are *you* phoning from? . . . St Paul's? Right, well get a taxi and come straight here." He hung up.

"Satisfied, Mr Holt?"

"I'm satisfied."

"Good. Now your side of the deal. Where's the key?"

Philip jerked his head at a pile of film plates and boxes scattered over the floor. "In one of those boxes."

"Don't waste my time. I've been through that lot"

"Not very thoroughly, though. One of the boxes has a small nick at the edge, made with a penknife. I fitted a false bottom to the box and filled it up with plates again."

"I'd have heard the key rattle," Fletcher said dubiously. "It's stuck to the false bottom."

With the gun pointing at Philip, Fletcher began sifting through the boxes. He gave a slight hiss as he found one with a tiny corner chipped off, and tugged at the box till the false bottom came free. The Yale key was neatly taped in place with adhesive tape.

"Ingenious," he muttered approvingly, pulling the key free and examining it carefully under the light. Then slowly an expression of fury spread over his swarthy features. "This is the one you had made? The copy of Mrs Curtis's?"

"Yes."

"Are you quite sure of that?"

"I give you my word."

Fletcher looked at the key again, spat out a violent oath, and flung it to the floor. Without another word he backed from the room, ran swiftly down the stairs, and into the street

Philip saw little point in trying to follow him; the Lancia was locked up in the garage and, in any case, Fletcher was armed. He might as well fill the time by clearing up the appalling mess. When Ruth's taxi drew up the office looked reasonably tidy.

He raced down to the street door. "Are you all right, Ruth? No broken bones, no bruises?"

She looked pale and dishevelled but managed an impudent smile. "All present and correct, sir! But you'll have to pay the taxi; they didn't give me time to take my handbag."

He did so and bounded up the stairs to join her in the office. "What the hell happened?"

She shrugged her shoulders. "Nothing much. A great hefty man pushed me into a car and dumped me in some sort of warehouse till your phone call came, that's all."

"And they didn't knock you about?"

"No. All I got was a ladder in my stocking when I tried to make a dash for it, and I seem to have lost my bracelet." Philip handed it to her and she smiled ruefully. "The original idea of these things was that they were supposed to bring good luck to the wearer. What was the shemozzle all about, anyway?"

Philip peered about the floor till he found the key Fletcher had thrown down. "This. You can add it to your charm bracelet. It appears that Fletcher doesn't want it after all. God knows why."

He explained the full sequence of events, starting with his visit to the El Barbecue coffee bar, and finally, gave an account of his eerie walk through the rain-sodden woods on Blackgate Common.

Ruth listened intently, then said, "I guessed you were up to something important when you marched out with that briefcase, but I assure you *I* didn't telephone Hyde. I didn't know where you were going, and I most certainly didn't know you were going to be murdered."

"Then who could the unknown lady have been? I'd like to thank her."

"It's obviously someone who wishes you well."

"Or wishes Clare Seldon evil," Philip remarked. "I've been thinking about it during the drive back. It seems a reasonable theory that Clare Seldon hired Fletcher to finish me off, only some unknown person stepped in and it was the Seldon woman who got killed instead."

"It sounds possible. But why should Clare Seldon suddenly become a target?"

"Perhaps she got too big for her boots. Perhaps she'd simply served her purpose in the set-up that she and Rex and Andy were obviously mixed up in."

"Luther Harris is mixed up in it too, don't forget. It was he who steered you to the El Barbecue where Mrs Seldon contacted you. I can't understand why Inspector Hyde doesn't slap Harris in jail."

"You can't put a man in jail merely on grounds of suspicion, my dear girl. As far as I can gather he's done his share of grilling

Luther, but it's my guess that he prefers to have the little chap running around loose, in the hope that he'll do something foolish and lead us on to big things."

"I hadn't thought of it like that How about the book Clare Seldon wanted so badly – have you still got it?"

"Yes, it's in the glove compartment of the car. We'll take another look at it later on."

"Aren't you going to phone Hyde about our latest little escapade?"

Philip looked at his watch. "It's getting pretty late. He'll have his hands full out at Blackgate Common just now, and, anyway, there's really very little to tell him. It'll save till tomorrow morning. What we both need is a square meal and a good night's rest, so that we have our brains dear to think this case out with Hyde tomorrow."

"You mean you want me to go to Scotland Yard with you?"

Philip grinned. "Yes, though it'll be like putting the cat among the pigeons, if you start flashing those saucy green eyes of yours at every detective you meet"

"It sounds loaded with possibilities," Ruth replied with a laugh. "I can hardly wait!"

It was, however, a very demure Ruth who sat across the mahogany desk from Inspector Hyde at Scotland Yard the following morning and gave her sober account of the abduction.

Hyde looked harassed and very tired, but there was an unmistakable warmth and admiration in his voice as he questioned her. "You did, in fact, put up quite a fight, Miss Sanders?"

"Oh, nothing much. There was a bit of a scuffle, that's all. When I saw this great big chap at the door I realised it was a mistake to have answered the bell, so I kicked him in the stomach—"

"You did *what?*" Philip cried.

" – and tried to slam the door. Unfortunately he got his foot in first, so I stamped on that, and I was wearing pretty sharp heels so he howled like a baby, and I ran up the stairs and made a dive for the telephone. That must have been when I tore my stocking. He came after me before I could dial 999 so I hit him in the face with the receiver—"

"Ruth! You never told me this!" Philip protested.

" – and I suppose that's when my charm bracelet snapped. Anyway, a fat lot of good it did me. Someone came up behind me and slapped a pad of chloroform over my nose and I can just remember being dragged outside and put in their car."

"Do you think you'd recognise any of these hooligans again, Miss Sanders?" Hyde inquired anxiously.

She shrugged her shoulders. "The one who rang the bell, perhaps. He was my jailer in the empty warehouse where they took me. He was fat and hideous, and he spoke with a slight West Country accent. He had an ex-Army issue overcoat and pointed shoes."

Hyde made notes as Ruth gave him details.

"The warehouse must have been near a tube station, I think – I felt the trains rumbling underneath. They came to a stop and started again, so it must have been a station. Probably somewhere near the Thames because I thought I could smell the river; and when they blindfolded me and pushed me into the car it took seven minutes to reach the call-box near St Paul's where they let me phone you. I looked at my watch, so I'm sure about the time."

Hyde's eyebrows were raised in appreciation. "Really, Miss Sanders, I think we could use you on the Force. All this might come in extremely useful. You have an exceptional young lady here, Mr Holt."

"Yes, it's slowly penetrating my solid skull, Inspector." Ruth blushed. "Can't we stop talking about me and get down to business? What's your opinion about the book, Inspector? 'Hier ist das Buch das Du brauchst.'"

"I'm still waiting for the graphologists to tell me if it's Linderhof's writing or not, Miss Sanders. I suspect it may have been a forgery to lure Mr Holt out to Blackgate Common."

"Where Fletcher was supposed to murder him?"

"Fletcher or someone else."

"Why someone else? It must have been Fletcher! Mr Holt told you about the mud on his shoes."

"All of London's parks and squares were muddy last night, Miss Sanders. Things would be different if we'd managed to pick Fletcher up there and then and have the mud analysed." The Inspector began to fill his pipe.

Ruth shook her head like an impatient terrier. "Well, if we can't pin anything on Mack-the-Knife, don't you think a few questions put to Luther Harris might produce results? After all, it *was* his tip about the Knightsbridge coffee bar that nearly led Philip into that terrible trap."

Hyde nodded patiently. "Harris is a rogue, and sooner or later he'll have to answer for his sins. He's not, however, the top man, I'm quite certain. Until the right moment comes I'm letting him roam around loose. With any luck at all he'll do something really foolish and lead us straight to the top."

"And you've still no idea who my anonymous benefactress is?" Philip asked. "The lady who phoned you about my going out to Blackgate Common?"

"No, I'm afraid the call can't be traced."

"I suppose you'll accuse me of being impatient again, Inspector," Ruth said, "but I fail to understand why you don't just haul in Fletcher and accuse him of about a dozen murders?'

"I wish it were as easy as that, Miss Sanders. In the first case, we haven't got him. We've spread a wide net for him, but so far he's managed to slip through it. Secondly, there's little doubt that he'll have staged a watertight alibi at one of his Chelsea clubs; this is no floundering amateur we're dealing with, you know." The Inspector blew out a cloud of smoke and studied it critically, then continued, "What really puzzles me is his obsession with the key. I mean, after going to such inordinate lengths to get hold of it I just can't understand why he should throw it away in disgust."

"Maybe it wasn't the one he wanted," Ruth suggested. "Well, it must have been," said Philip.

"Not necessarily. There were two, weren't there? The original, and the duplicate you had cut at Windsor. One you handed in to the Inspector, and—"

"Yes, but the duplicate was an exact copy of the original, there's not a shadow of doubt about that."

Inspector Hyde placed his pipe in an ashtray and leant forward. "Do you have the key with you, Mr Holt?"

Philip nodded and produced the key, while Hyde delved in a drawer and took out a glossy photoprint. "As you know," he said, "I returned the original key to Mrs Curtis, as it was undoubtedly her property; but I had some pictures taken, just for the record."

He laid the print alongside the key Philip had handed him and studied them carefully under a magnifying glass.

"They're absolutely the same in every respect . . . except for – Good heavens! Talk about not seeing the wood for the trees! I've been concentrating on the cut, but it hasn't got anything to do with that. Look for yourselves."

Philip and Ruth craned eagerly forward.

"I still don't get it," said Ruth.

"Wait a moment. *The numbers!*" Philip said tensely.

"Exactly! There are no numbers on the duplicate. But there *are* on the original. It wasn't the key itself Fletcher was after, it was the serial number on the key. This is probably the missing part of the code."

Philip said, "I don't get you. What code?"

"You remember the accordion photographs?"

"How could I forget them?" Philip muttered wryly.

"Quite so. Well, acting on a hunch I sent them down to our Code Department and asked them to work on them. The word came back that this was all very nice but could they please have the other half of the code? Then the pattern might begin to make sense, they said." The Inspector reached for the telephone on his desk "I sent them the Belloc poems, but they shot that back in my lap and assured me I was on the wrong . . . Hello, Hyde speaking. Get me Major Osborne please."

"Inspector, how can there be a code in a bunch of accordion photographs?" Ruth asked.

"The position of the fingers, Miss Sanders. Mrs Stansdale was photographed by Quayle and Fletcher with her fingers placed differently on the accordion keyboard in each shot. And we think that each photograph represented either a number or a note of music. Fletcher probably thought Quayle was taking him completely into his confidence, whereas in actual fact Quayle was concealing the vital significance of his sister's apartment key – the other part of the code. I think that's why Quayle and Fletcher fell out. Fletcher has certainly been moving heaven and earth since then to get . . ." He broke off and spoke into the telephone. "Hello, Major Osborne? . . . Oh . . . Inspector Hyde here. Will you ask him to ring me the moment he gets back? Thank you."

The Inspector looked fleetingly disappointed, then rose and paced the room. Eventually he stopped and faced Philip. "Mr Holt, leaving aside your lapse of last night, does our treaty of co-operation still hold good?"

"It most certainly does. But I warn you, I'm just not on the ball about this code business. The code to what?"

"I'm not one hundred per cent certain yet. We'll know when Major Osborne and his eggheads get busy. However, it may take them some little time to crack it, and I don't think we should sit here cooling our heels until they do. I have a suggestion to make – a trifle unorthodox, I'm afraid . . ."

"I'm all in favour of the unorthodox, Inspector," Philip said with a grin.

Hyde coughed discreetly. "Er . . . yes, so I've noticed. Well, what I want you to do is go and see Corporal Wilson in hospital."

"What's so unusual about that?"

"The visit itself – nothing. It's what you will tell him that is slightly irregular. That's why only you can do it. I, as an official person, am barred."

"That sounds fascinating. What do I tell him?"

"Listen carefully," said the Inspector as he took his place behind the desk and outlined his plan.

Chapter Thirteen

"Andy, have you ever heard of Scylla and Charybdis?" Philip asked as the sullen eyes in the corner bed of the hospital ward continued to avoid him.

"Who's that? A new beat group?"

"No. Scylla and Charybdis were two famous monsters in Greek mythology. They used to hang out on a couple of rocks on either side of a narrow strait, somewhere between Italy and Sicily. The sailors who passed between those rocks did so at peril to their lives."

"What's all that got to do with me?"

"I'm just drawing a picture for you, showing how it's going to be when you go sailing out of this hospital in a week or two."

"I don't need you to draw no pictures for me."

"Yes, you do. You're going right down that narrow strait between your own private Scylla and Charybdis, and I don't give much for your chances."

"I can take care of myself, mate."

"Can you? I have my doubts about that, Andy. It seems to me, with the position you're in, you won't last long. It'll either be the six-headed monster – 'the desperate people' who tried to kill you, and have already killed Rex, and Quayle, and Clare Seldon – or on the other side of the strait you'll get sucked into the whirlpool the police have got ready for you. You're going to need some friends, Andy, some real friends, when that time comes. Don't have any illusions about Inspector Hyde. He may have eased off the pressure while you were a sick man on the danger list, but believe me he's going to come down on you like a ton of bricks as soon as you walk out of this ward. Now that they've got Fletcher there's no holding the man."

"They've got who?"

"Fletcher. They picked him up yesterday," Philip lied. "I tell you, there's no stopping Hyde now; he's like a steam-train tearing down the track with the throttle wide open. I don't think he expected a type like Fletcher to crack so easily, but you know how it is – when these so-called big shots get the wind up they'll say anything to save their own skins."

Small globules of sweat had begun to break out on Andy's thin pate, and he licked his lips with a dry tongue. "Damned if I know what you're talking about, mate! I've never heard of any Fletcher."

Philip snorted derisively. "Come off it, Andy! The most senile judge in the world won't believe that, not after he's listened to Fletcher's testimony. Mind you, I dare say half the things he's saying about you aren't true. I mean, it's obvious he's doing his level best to incriminate just about everybody in order to take the limelight off himself, but he's said enough about you and Rex to send you up for—"

"The dirty, double-crossing swine!" Andy hissed. "I knew I shouldn't have trusted him."

Philip's heart skipped a beat. It was the breakthrough they had hoped for. He steeled himself to appear utterly casual "No, you certainly slipped up there, old chap," he agreed cordially, picking up a magazine from the locker and idly flicking through it "How did you come to meet a type like that in the first place?"

"Well . . . we was in a strip-joint in Soho, Rex and me. Cliff bumped into us quite by accident. I hadn't seen him for some time. He . . . er . . . well, he and I did a few little deals together in the past – some Army supplies I was able to – to get hold of."

"Don't tell me Fletcher was in the Army?"

"No. But I was. And he was able to dispose of the stuff in Civvy Street. Between us we made quite a nice little bit on the side. I hadn't seen him since those days. Hey, wait a moment! Why am I telling you all this? I thought you said Fletcher had already—"

"There just hasn't been time to hear the full story, old chap," Philip said swiftly. "Hyde would need at least a month for that." It was touch and go whether Andy would believe him. He would have to risk his major arrow into the blue. "What Hyde is after is the truth about the Hamburg Bank job."

Fear flickered like summer lightning in Andy's eyes; the arrow had struck home.

Philip quelled the inner surge of excitement and went on casually, "If one were to believe Fletcher, it was you who just about organised the whole job."

"The bloody liar! Rex and me was just a couple of stooges. If we hadn't been in debt to him like we was we wouldn't never have done it."

"Debt? So he had his claws into you! How did that happen?"

"Like I said, we bumped into him at this strip joint. We had a few drinks, then he invited us to a real plush place where the birds weren't all tarts and the booze was genuine. It was a bit out of my class, really, but Rex liked it and of course the dames all liked him, so I sort of strung along. I didn't get much kick out of things until later on, when Cliff took us into a private room at the back. They was playing cards. I've won a few quid at cards in my time, so I was keen to have a go. We won the best part of eighty quid between us. We was tickled pink."

"How long did the eighty pounds last?"

Andy managed a rueful smile. "You know Rex – money went through his fingers like water. Women, booze, jazz records. I wasn't far behind him myself. A couple of days later we was back at the card table, and Cliff all smiles and acting Santa Claus when we needed a stake."

"How much did you lose?"

"Nearly six hundred quid."

"Oh, my God! And Fletcher took your I.O.U.s, I suppose?"

Andy nodded.

Philip flung the magazine on to the bed. "Why the hell didn't Rex come to me? I'd have found the money somewhere."

Andy squirmed uncomfortably but made no reply.

"How long was it before Fletcher began to put the pressure on you?"

"Not long. Just before our leave came to an end. He knew we was stationed in Hamburg and he told us we needn't pay him back, provided we did a little service for him. We was to get friendly with a chap called Weston."

"The cashier at the bank in Hamburg?"

"Yes."

"He was an Englishman doing a twelve-month stint on some exchange scheme, wasn't he?"

"That's right. It didn't take us long to get to know him. Cliff had tipped us off that Weston knew about the transfer of a ruddy great pile of lolly from the Hamburg bank to a big engineering works at Düsseldorf. All we had to do was find out when and how the transfer was going to take place. If we got that information for him we'd get a nice cut from the hijacking which Cliff was planning, and he'd tear up our I.O.U.s as well. It sounded simple enough. Like I said, there was no rough stuff involved, only a bit of information."

"Unfortunately Weston got himself killed, didn't he?"

"Yes. Honest, Philip, we didn't have nothing to do with that side of things, word of honour!"

Philip studied him carefully for a moment "I believe you, Andy, but I'm not sure Hyde will. Fletcher's singing a different tune down at Scotland Yard."

Andy's comment on Cliff Fletcher would have made a bargee blench.

"Quite so," said Philip, consciously imitating one of Inspector Hyde's mannerisms. "What happened then?"

"Well, they brought the job off and managed to fly the lolly over to England in a private freight plane. I never did find out exactly how much it was, but I reckon it wasn't much short of a million marks."

"And Fletcher tore up your I.O.U.s?"

"Yes, but we didn't get the cut that was promised us. There was a hitch somewhere."

"What do you mean, there was a hitch?"

"Someone up top was sitting on the lolly and it didn't look as though we was going to get our share."

"Just where did Luther Harris fit into all this?"

"He was the go-between whenever we needed to contact Fletcher. We wasn't encouraged to get in touch with Cliff direct."

"I see. Go on."

"Well, we began to get impatient, so we put the pressure on Luther. Things began to look more promising when Luther passed on the word from Cliff; Rex was to go and stay at the Royal Falcon Hotel in Maidenhead and wait until the organisation contacted him."

"So *that* was what he was doing there! Waiting for pay day."

"Yes. And that book of poetry he was carrying around was a sign to show that everything was going according to plan; Rex was told to use it as his means of identifying himself."

"Wait a moment, Andy. Why should Rex need to identify himself? Fletcher knew what Rex looked like."

"It wasn't Fletcher who was to pay out the lolly."

"Who was it, then?"

"I dunno. Like I said, we was the stooges, we vvasn't allowed to know too much. Fletcher never did let on who he was taking his orders fromn. Anyway, Rex must have got on the wrong side of sotnebody up top and they murdered him."

"What an appalling mess!"

"It didn't seem like it at the time. We thought it was all dead easy."

A bitter retort was on the tip of Philip's tongue but he bit it back. Getting Andy riled at this moment would serve no good purpose; there was a great deal of information still to be sweated out of him if he were patient

"One thing I don't get, Andy. Why did you pinch that book of poetry from my studio?"

" 'Cos I reckoned that if I had that book the big shot with the money would get in touch with me and pay what was due to us."

"Rather naïve of you, wasn't it? Instead of that they nearly shot you dead, because you'd served your purpose and knew just a little too much."

Andy fidgeted in his bed and wiped the perspiration from his scalp.

"Have you any idea who might have been behind the attempt to shoot you?"

"Like I say, I don't know who's giving the orders up top. I knew what Rex was waiting for at the hotel, so maybe whoever it was thought I'd go and squeal to the rozzers. But one thing I'm fairly certain about – it was true about the dough. Someone *was* hiding it and wouldn't say where. The chap who might have known was that pansy. Quayle. Or Mrs Curtis's lover-boy, Talbot."

"You mean the hotel manager?"

Andy nodded. "She was his mistress all right. Hadn't you worked that one out?"

"M'm . . ." murmured Philip reflectively. "Quayle certainly knew where the money was, since he was the one who thought up the code . . ."

"Has Cliff squealed about that too?"

"No, actually we were able to work that one out ourselves, with the aid of the key and the photographs," Philip replied glibly, wondering whether Major Osborne's department had in fact succeeded in cracking it.

A tiny flicker of greed showed in the sick man's eyes. "I'd give a tidy bit to find out where the hiding place is," he hinted heavily.

Philip looked at him in blank astonishment. It was incredible! After coming within a hairbreadth of losing his life, the unclaimed money could still remain a tantalising obsession to him. Suddenly the atmosphere at Andy's bedside grew too much for Philip and he found himself longing for fresh air. He stood up.

"You'll put in a good word for me, like you said, Philip?"

"I'll do what I can."

"We didn't do nothing, only pass on a bit of information."

Philip regarded him with disgust. On the tip of his tongue was the angry accusation that by his greed he had managed to sway a weak character like Rex and bring about his death, and the death of a bank cashier, and cause endless worry and heartbreak in a score of places. But he bit on his tongue. "No, Andy," he remarked thinly, "you haven't done anything."

He turned on his heel and walked through the ward and out into the sunshine that was bathing Goodge Street in pale yellow light. Hailing a passing taxi – his Lancia was in at the garage for an oil change – he ordered the driver to take him to Scotland Yard.

"Illuminating, isn't it, Mr Holt?" Inspector Hyde had listened carefully as Philip recounted Andy's sordid tale. "So he fell for the idea of Fletcher's having turned Queen's Evidence?"

Philip nodded. "Hook, line, and sinker. I think the picture of Fletcher being under lock and key gave him added confidence to make a clean breast of things. Mind you, the man's a congenital liar, so I don't suppose we can believe everything he told me, and he'll probably retract every word of it once he finds out that Fletcher isn't in the bag."

"Nevertheless, he's given us plenty to go on, and it all fits in with what we knew and what we surmised. The exasperating thing is, we still don't know where the money is hidden. Nor do we really know whose brains are at the top of the organisation."

"The finger seems to point to the Royal Falcon, if you ask me. We know from what Linderhof told us that Mrs Curtis is involved in some way."

'Either she or Talbot could have murdered your brother, certainly. There was ample opportunity. But I'd be inclined to think the master-mind was probably Thomas Quayle."

"Then why was he killed?"

"I think . . . I'm not sure, mind, but I think because he was sitting on the money and refused to share out. And he was the only person who knew the exact hiding-place."

"Luther Harris must have been a smart lad, to have siphoned off his share before the rest went off the market," said Philip. "I still don't quite grasp what he hoped to gain by handing it back to you on a silver platter."

"Oh, I think he got cold feet after seeing his name on that dance ticket. He was probably hoping that if he got rid of his share and at the same time managed to weight the suspicion against Wilson, then both the police and Fletcher's party might ignore him. Actually, when you analyse it I think you'll find it's the old, old story of when thieves fall out . . ."

"Yes. Tell me, is there no sign of life from your Code Department yet?"

For answer the Inspector drew his scribbling block towards him. "There are signs of life, but they don't make sense. Major Osborne has the notion that the code word, made up from the numbers on the key and the Stansdale photographs, is 'Venice'. Simply one word – 'Venice'. It's so depressing; it's a huge city, there must be a million hiding places. Just where should we start looking?"

"Venice!" Philip ejaculated, a gleam of recognition slowly stirring on his face.

Hyde looked at him with interest.

Philip's fingers drummed a nervous tattoo on the edge of the mahogany desk. "I don't know. It's . . . it's too far-fetched. Besides, you've already searched the place."

"What place, Mr Holt?"

"The shop. Quayle's antique shop at Brighton . . . Look, I know this may sound silly, but I remember noticing a great chest there – it was marked SOLD. There was a painting reproduced on the lid. The scene was *St Mark's Square, Venice.*"

Hyde sat upright. "I wonder . . . !"

Philip sought to dismiss the notion. "Of course, the idea's absurd! The local police will have combed the place from top to bottom."

"Then they can damn well comb it again!" Hyde seized the phone. "It would be just like that fellow Lang to have slipped up on a thing like that. Get me Inspector Lang!" he barked into the phone.

He had scarcely replaced the receiver when the telephone rang. He looked surprised; it was too soon for the call to Brighton to have come through.

"Hyde speaking . . . Oh, hello, Sergeant . . . Where? . . . Maidenhead . . . Are you sure? . . . When did it happen? . . . Who identified the body, then? . . . I see . . . No, don't do that. I'm just waiting for a phone call and then I'll come down right away."

He slammed down the receiver, stood up, and snatched his hat and raincoat from the stand.

"Our thieves still appear to be falling out. Douglas Talbot has been murdered. Someone's battered his face in and dumped the body in a ditch two hundred yards from the Royal Falcon Hotel."

Chapter Fourteen

Thieves had indeed fallen out, Hyde reflected grimly, as he examined the mutilated body of Douglas Talbot. In the chain-fission of ugly murders which the thieves had touched off, this last killing was quite the most brutal. Scarcely any feature of the once impeccably groomed hotel manager's face was recognisable. If it had not been for his clothes and the diary in his jacket pocket the local police would have had nothing to go on in their task of identifying the corpse. The diary, however, issued by a large firm of caterers, had borne his name, and the tailor's tag inside his well-cut suit had confirmed it. They had fetched Mrs Curtis from the Royal Falcon, and she had fainted on the spot when she had seen the corpse.

Inspector Hyde was faced with the unenviable task of interrogating Mrs Curtis. Pale, and more than ever like a frightened little bird, it was only with difficulty that she was able to frame more or less coherent answers to his questions.

"Tell me, Mrs Curtis," Hyde was saying gently, "did Mr Talbot say he was going out at all?"

"Yes. He left early and said he—"

"Early today, or yesterday?"

"Early this morning. It was that man, I'm sure."

"What man, Mrs Curtis?"

"The man he was going to meet"

"He had an appointment, then?"

"Yes. He had an appointment with a Mr Fletcher."

"I see . . ." The Inspector held Talbot's pocket diary in his hand; the appointment with Fletcher was confirmed, in Talbot's neat handwriting, in the space allotted for that day's date. "This man Fletcher – have you met him?"

"No, never. All I know is that Douglas talked to him on the telephone once or twice."

"There's an entry in the diary showing that Talbot had an appointment with him today. Have you any idea where they were supposed to meet?"

"None at all, I'm afraid."

"Did he say when he was likely to be back?"

"Who? Mr Fletcher?"

"No, Mrs Curtis; did Mr Talbot say when he was likely to be back?"

"Yes. That's to say, he didn't. I mean, not until this evening."

Under cover of filling his pipe Inspector Hyde studied Vanessa Curtis. A large part of her distraught, perpetually flustered manner was genuine, he was sure of that. But all of it? It seemed to him that there was a quality of fear and evasiveness which had lain hidden before but was now, despite her frantic efforts to suppress it, protruding rather sharply. One of the more unpleasant aspects of his duty was that he was obliged to question bereaved relatives and close friends immediately after an accident or crime had occurred; and he was not a hard man by nature. However, there were times when one had to be hard in order to achieve results.

"Mrs Curtis," Hyde went on "this must be a shocking blow to you and to the hotel. You have my fullest sympathy, and I very much regret the fact that I have to bother you with questions now. However, if we're to get to the bottom of this callous murder you'll have to help."

The little woman winced and played even more distractedly with the frills of her-lace jabot, then took out a tiny handkerchief and began to twist it constantly round her fingers.

"Now, when I was first called in to investigate the suicide of Rex Holt I naturally talked to Mr Talbot, and it was also my job to instigate some private inquiries about him."

Mrs Curtis gave him a look of pure fright.

"What struck me as rather unusual was the speed with which Mr Talbot appeared to learn the hotel trade. He was on the Stock Exchange, I believe, at the time your husband was killed?"

"Er . . . yes, that's correct."

"And he had never had anything to do with the hotel business before?"

"That's not true. He came in here often."

"Quite so. But as a guest, surely? I doubt whether one can learn to manage an hotel by simply dropping in from time to time for a drink at the bar."

Mrs Curtis made no answer.

"Now I found it a little odd that within one year of your husband's death Mr Talbot had succeeded in firmly establishing himself as your manager."

"You don't understand . . . I was very ill, I didn't know which way to turn, I had to have someone."

"Then why didn't you engage a trained manager? I'm assured that there's no shortage of qualified people."

"I . . . I knew Douglas, and he was . . . well, he was so very efficient"

"I agree that he was a very strong personality, Mrs Curtis. A person you found difficulty in saying no to, is that it?"

"Yes," she said in a low voice.

"I wonder whether you'd care to enlarge on your personal relationship towards Mr Talbot?"

"Personal relationship? What do you mean?"

"Please be frank with me, Mrs Curtis. It will save such a lot of time."

"I was his employer. I told him what I wanted done and—"

"I'm sorry, Mrs Curtis, but my observations and information don't support that statement. I believe it was Mr Talbot who gave the orders?"

"I was still the owner—"

"In name only, I suggest"

"You don't understand . . . I wasn't well, my nerves were ragged and—"

"And Douglas Talbot saw this and assumed complete control of your affairs. Am I right, Mrs Curtis?"

For a moment longer she held out; then she gave a slight nod of the head and gulped convulsively. "Yes," she whispered.

Hyde recognised the breakthrough. It was not the moment to be weak. "I don't think it ended there, did it?" he pressed relentlessly. "Please tell me the truth. Was Mr Talbot your lover?"

Vanessa Curtis began sobbing, but she nodded an affirmative.

"What it boils down to is that he used his considerable physical charm and his dominating personality to obtain complete control over your business and emotional life."

Hyde's harsh statement seemed to help her face reality, perhaps for the first time. Dabbing her eyes with the handkerchief she answered him almost calmly. "Yes, Douglas used me. I didn't realise it at first. I thought he was genuinely fond of me. And when my husband died, I . . . I needed somebody. By the time I found out what he was really like – cold, ruthless, calculating – it was too late. I've known for some time that he was finished with me, that he was interested in another woman. I was too dowdy for him, too provincial. He wanted something smarter." It was on the tip of the Inspector's tongue to ask, "Clare Seldon?" But he refrained. He knew it was vital, now that the little woman's defences were broken down, to press on with the main drive of his questioning.

"What happened when Rex Holt stayed here, Mrs Curtis?"

She shook her head in bewilderment, genuinely unable to cope with the complications of the case. "I don't know very much. I wasn't told exactly what was going on. All I know is that Douglas and my brother Thomas were connected in some kind of business or other. I got the impression that a lot of money was involved. Douglas was money-mad, he said the only true power in the world was money."

"And he was a power-greedy man."

"Yes . . . yes, that's absolutely true. I mean, he didn't want money for what it could buy, such as to travel abroad, or a big car, or nice possessions, he wanted it for its own sake, because he would wield power with it."

"Your brother Thomas was hardly that sort of man, though, was he?"

"No. Thomas was very different. He wanted money, but it was so that he could buy beautiful things with it – things he was too lazy to work for and earn. He considered it an outrage that a person of his tastes and sensibilities had to work for a living. He thought that all the fine things of life should be his by right."

Inspector Hyde nodded. He was inwardly surprised at her intelligent appraisal of the characters of Talbot and Quayle. During his own search for motives he had mentally linked the two men and had found difficulty in imagining what their common bond might be.

"You were going to tell me what happened to Rex Holt," he pursued, quietly.

"He was murdered."

"By Talbot?"

"I'm not certain. All I know is that Douglas ordered me to go to Mr Holt's room that night and try to persuade him to stay. Mr Holt had been waiting at the hotel for something – I think it was a large sum of money – and his patience was running out. He insisted on leaving and got very angry. I left his room, went back to Douglas and told him that I hadn't been successful in persuading Mr Holt to stay. Douglas flew into a terrible rage."

"Did he frequently lose his temper?"

"Often."

"Was he physically violent? I'm sorry to have to ask it, but did he ever . . . ?"

"Yes, he knocked me about from time to time."

"Charming fellow. Apart from the fact that one doesn't hit the gentle sex, he must have been at least twice your weight and very nearly twice your height"

Vanessa Curtis shrugged indifferently.

"So it's a fair supposition that Talbot went to Holt's room later that night, under cover of the noisy Dramatic Society's banquet, quarrelled with him, shot him, and then faked a note to make it look like suicide."

"I don't know. I was never told, and I never dared ask. But I think it was something like that"

The Inspector stood up and paced the room. He was inclined to think that Mrs Curtis was telling the truth, as far as she knew it. He did not think there was any more she had to tell him about Rex Holt

After a while he resumed his seat and took out Talbot's pocket diary. "What about the telephone numbers at the back of this book?" said Hyde, passing her the diary. "Do they mean anything to you?"

She took it and stared at the list of numbers. "They're mostly local tradesmen – our wine merchants . . . the butcher . . . people in the Maidenhead district whom we do business with. I don't know about the London numbers – probably some of his women friends," she added bitterly.

He was silent as she continued looking at the book.

"Wait a moment, here's one I know. A London number. He rang that one quite often. It's a music shop in Tottenham Court Road, owned by a fat little man named Luther Harris."

"I see. And none of the other numbers has any special significance for you?"

"No, I don't think so?'

"Thank you." Hyde stood up and slipped the diary into his briefcase.

Mrs Curtis was eyeing him furtively, wondering if she dared hope that he was about to leave. He was, but he had not quite finished with her. Despite the measure of genuine pity he felt for her, he knew it would be a mistake to be too kind. There were certain women in life who made a very successful thing out of trading on their apparent helplessness and feminine frailty; if his guess was right this was the unknown female voice on the telephone, the person who had probably persuaded Fletcher to change his allegiance and murder Clare Seldon instead of Philip Holt at Blackgate Common. She probably knew more about Talbot's activities than she had so far admitted. Even now she might be capable of some obstructive action, just when the last delicate scene of the drama was about to be played.

He remained in the doorway and spoke in serious tones. "Mrs Curtis, I think I ought to make clear to you the gravity of your position. By your own admission you are guilty of the offence of withholding information from the police; I refer to your conversation with Rex Holt in Room 27, under Talbot's orders. There are other matters, too, in which I fear you haven't been entirely frank with me. I suggest you now do nothing – nothing at all, do you understand? – which might in any way worsen your situation. No telephone calls, no letters, no attempt to communicate with anyone who is or was in any fashion connected with this case. Have I made myself quite clear?"

Vanessa Curtis took refuge in a flood of tears, but Hyde was fairly certain that his point had gone home.

He drove back to London. It was Luther Harris he had in mind, though he had not mentioned the name for fear of putting ideas into Vanessa Curtis's head. If Harris were to receive a warning at this stage it would torpedo the scheme taking shape in Hyde's mind.

The police car took him to Philip Holt's studios where Philip and Ruth were engaged in photographing a languid blonde who was modelling a twin-set.

"Did you ever see such a skinny clothes-horse in your life?" Ruth hissed to the Inspector, nodding towards the open door of the studio.

Hyde gave her a conspiratorial smile as Philip put his head round the edge of the door.

"Be with you in a moment, Inspector," Philip said. "Ruth will make you a cup of tea and entertain you while I'm finishing here."

"Thank you, but I've no time for tea, I'm afraid. It's actually Miss Sanders I came to see."

"Oh, really? You're not trying to enroll her in the Women's Police Force, are you? She's far too useful to me, you know."

Ruth grinned and closed the door between the studio and the office. "What can I do for you, Inspector?"

Quietly, so that he should not be overheard, Hyde said, "I want you to put a flea in a certain gentleman's ear."

"An attractive gentleman, I trust?"

"Mr Luther Harris."

Ruth's expression caused the Inspector to chuckle. "Duty before pleasure, Miss Sanders. Will you help me?"

"Of course. What do I have to do?"

"I want you to drop into Pop's Corner tomorrow morning, in a very casual sort of way. Maybe you're looking for a record for a jazz-hungry nephew or something. See if you can get chatting with Harris. You know him slightly, don't you?"

"Well enough, I should say. What's the flea I'm to put in his ear?"

"It concerns Quayle's antique shop at Brighton. I want Harris to know that we, the police, are suddenly interested in that shop again. Naturally, you'll bring this up in a roundabout fashion. Mention that you've heard that Douglas Talbot has been murdered – it'll be in the papers tomorrow. Then work your way round to telling him that I've been pestering Mr Holt with endless questions, asking what Mr. Holt was doing down at Quayle's antique shop that afternoon. You must casually let drop the fact that the police are investigating the Hamburg bank robbery, and that we think Talbot, Quayle, and Fletcher were mixed up in it. And then tell him that the code word which we've got hold of leads us to think that the bulk of the money is still hidden on Quayle's premises somewhere. Now have you got all that?"

"I think so. Just to make sure, would you go over it again?"

The Inspector complied, while Ruth listened carefully.

"Right, I've got it. Then I buy my jazz-hungry nephew his record and leave. What then?"

"Report back to me. Here's my number at the Yard. I'll be waiting to hear from you. When you've told me how it's gone you must return here in the normal way. Whatever you do, don't try to follow Harris or anything like that. Leave that side of things to us. All right?"

"It'll be a pleasure, Inspector," Ruth answered, her green eyes sparkling with excitement.

"Hyde speaking."

"It worked!" Ruth's voice bubbled over the telephone line. "At least, I think it did, Inspector."

"Splendid! What were Harris's reactions?"

"He's a cagey character, but I think I've whetted his appetite. He pretended not to be interested, but he kept on coming back to the listening booth where I was playing records and asking me questions. I should say the flea's in his ear all right."

"Well done! I really am most grateful to you. I knew I could rely on you."

"Any time, Inspector, any time at all. 'Bye now."

At midday the Inspector's phone rang again.

"Thompson here, sir. He's just dropping his shutters."

"Does he generally do that at lunch-time?"

"Not as a rule. Looks like he's shutting up for the day."

"Splendid. Don't let him out of your sight. And, Sergeant – be careful! You may not be the only one on his heels. I'll wait for your next report in the Radio Room."

"May I come too?" Philip asked.

Inspector Hyde looked at him and smiled. Either Ruth had tipped him off or some sixth sense had told him it might be interesting to pay the Yard a social call that morning. "Highly unorthodox, sir, but . . ."

"We were unorthodox a couple of days ago, remember? It paid off."

"Very well, Mr Holt. I might as well be hung for a sheep as a lamb."

They hurried down to the Radio Room and spent an anxious five minutes till the crackle of Sergeant Thompson's special car transmitter came on the air.

"I'm trailing two cars over Waterloo Bridge. Luther Harris

is in the first one, a new beige-and-green Zodiac. The car on his tail is a T.R.4, red-and-black, with the hood up. I haven't been able to spot who's in it yet. Here are the number-plates: Zodiac . . ."

A police assistant wrote the numbers down, Hyde acknowledged the call, and Thompson went off the air.

"Do we tail him'?" Philip said eagerly. "My Lancia's got the legs of both . . ."

"No. It'll look like the London to Brighton Rally if we get on the road too. The Brighton Belle's due to leave shortly, if we hurry we can get it. Let's go!"

Inspector Lang was waiting at Brighton station when the famous express train drew in. It was a subdued Lang compared with the hearty, self-satisfied man who had conducted the inquiry into Thomas Quayle's death.

"You think we've slipped up somewhere?" he asked anxiously as Hyde squatted uncomfortably in the back of the innocuous-looking delivery van (with a specially souped-up engine) which was speeding them to the street where Quayle's shop stood.

"I'm not sure," Hyde replied shortly, "but it looks damn like it. Anyway, we'll cry about spilt milk afterwards. The chief thing now is, have you got everything laid on properly on this job?"

"I think so. My team are all in plain-clothes, and they've had strict instructions to keep out of sight till you give the word. There's an empty house more or less opposite the shop. We can watch the proceedings from there."

"If we get there first," Hyde grimly reminded him.

They did. The innocent-looking delivery van disgorded them in front of a large old-fashioned house opposite Quayle's shop and drove swiftly away. Lang produced an estate agent's key and quickly led the way to an empty room on the ground floor.

They concealed themselves behind half-drawn, musty-smelling curtains, and took up their watch. Out of the corner of his eye Hyde was aware that Philip was fingering an object in his jacket pocket.

"You're not carrying a gun, are you, Mr Holt?" he murmured quietly. "You leave the rough stuff to us, that's what we're paid for."

Philip smiled engagingly. "Me, carry a gun, Inspector? I wouldn't dream of such a thing!"

They didn't have to wait long. A moment later a green-and-beige Zodiac swung round the far corner of the street and cruised slowly past the antique shop. Luther Harris peered from the driver's seat, scanning to right and left.

"He's taking no chances," Hyde muttered. "I hope to heaven your men keep out of sight"

"They'd better!" Lang growled. "Or we'll all be out of a job when this is over."

Apparently satisfied, Luther Harris made a U-turn and drove back to the shop.

Philip moved to a well-concealed point of vantage, drew his Olympus Pen F from his pocket, and, at the critical moment when Luther stepped out of the car, clicked the shutter. "One more for my Rogues' Gallery. Should there be any slip up, at least he can't deny he was here," Philip whispered.

Hyde grunted his approval.

Luther produced a key and, glancing once more up and down the street, let himself into the shop.

"Quite at home, isn't he?" Hyde observed. "I wonder where he got the key from?"

They did not see the T.R.4 arrive. Its driver had evidently taken the precaution of parking out of sight. A tall, saturnine figure in a belted raincoat, with a snap-brim hat pulled down over his eyes, appeared within their range of vision.

As Hyde hissed, *Fletcher!* Philip aimed the tiny camera and clicked the shutter again.

Fletcher gave scarcely a glance at the parked Zodiac. As he reached the shop he slipped quickly down the iron steps and let himself into the basement.

"Do we go in?" Lang whispered tensely.

Hyde shook his head. "We'll give them a couple of minutes to pass the time of day and find the money for us, then you can give the signal."

The second hand on Hyde's watch ticked forward. A minute passed. All was silent in the drab, curving street. Slowly the three men rose from their crouching positions. Lang lifted his eyebrows in silent inquiry, and Hyde frowned at the man's impatience. The seconds dragged by.

Then at last Hyde nodded. "Okay. We close in."

At that moment all hell broke loose. There was a muffled report from a gun, a door slammed, a stifled cry of anguish cut the quiet air, then there was the sound of feet pounding up the iron staircase and a second later Fletcher came into view.

With a suppressed oath Philip flung up the sash window in front of him and vaulted over the ledge. He was halfway across the road before Fletcher saw him coming. Fletcher yelled with rage and began to run as a shrill cacophony of police whistles shredded the air. As if by magic the street was suddenly filled with muscular plain-clothes policemen.

Fletcher slithered to a halt, spun round, and plucked frantically in his raincoat pocket for his gun. He tried to swerve as he saw Philip coming at him, but he was a second too late. Philip hurled himself like a torpedo at the pit of Fletcher's stomach, sending the gun spinning in a wide arc across the street. Philip rolled on to his feet with astonishing agility and retrieved the gun, but precautions were no longer necessary. Fletcher lay doubled up, all wind and fight knocked out of him.

Hyde came up at a smart pace and snapped handcuffs on the gasping man. He took the gun from Philip and snarled at Fletcher, "What's the trouble, Sandman – have you run out of knives?"

The caustic remark was deadly accurate. Fletcher's habitual weapon was found embedded in the body of Luther Harris, alongside a large chest with a fine Canaletto painting on the lid. The chest had been opened and the false bottom smashed to splinters by a heavy antique sabre.

Inspector Lang stared at the chest. "How the devil did we manage to miss that!"

Hyde gave him a bleak look, but made no comment; it was small consolation that his origina estimate of Lang's slipshod methods had proved correct. Of far greater importance was the fact that the money had gone. A swift search of Fletcher and of Luther Harris's body failed to turn up a single German mark.

Someone had got in ahead of them. Who?

Hyde, not usually a man to place faith in hunches, hoped profoundly that the hunch he had now would prove right.

Chapter Fifteen

Philip flopped into the chair behind his desk and reached for a cigarette.

"Put that coffin nail away!" Ruth ordered mildly.

"Don't you think I've earned at least one?"

"You've had a hard day down at Brighton, I'll grant you that," Ruth said. "But that's no excuse to come off the wagon again. I'll bet you chain-smoked in the train all the way up to Town."

Philip smiled ruefully: "I spiked my own guns by making Hyde come into a non-smoker with me. Anyway, I had no time, I was so busy answering his questions."

"Questions? Don't tell me the Inspector thinks *you've* got the money?"

"No . . . Though, mind you, he's got some pretty strange ideas in his head. I wouldn't blame him if he did think something like that. After all, somebody's got it tucked away somewhere."

"But who? And where? It's absolutely baffling. Quayle and Talbot are dead, so are Luther Harris and Clare Seldon; Fletcher's under lock and key, and Andy's in hospital, so he couldn't have spirited the German marks out of the chest. I mean, who is there left?"

"There's little Mrs Curtis, don't forget."

"Are you serious?"

"No, not really. If it were as simple as that the police would simply arrest her and force the truth out of her."

Ruth frowned in deep thought. "What did you mean just now when you said Hyde has some pretty strange ideas? Did he tell you something?"

"In a round-about way, yes." Philip paused, and pushing

his lighter out of arm's reach he put an unlit cigarette in his mouth.

Ruth bridled with impatience. "Oh, do stop being so cagey, Philip! What did he say?"

"Well, he seemed to think it would be a good idea if I did a photographic survey of the Ancient Inns of Britain."

Ruth stared. "Whatever for?"

"No, I didn't get the point either, at first. The old boy led up to it in a very round-about fashion. He said how impressed he and the general public had been with my work on Stratford-on-Avon and the Shakespeare Survey, and what a talent I had for spotting the unusual angle to a well-worn subject, and a load of similar blarney. It was all beautifully done; I think we'd passed through Three Bridges or even Redhill before he started dropping hints about his Ancient Inns scheme."

"And what is his Ancient Inns scheme? Do you mean to tell me he wants you to go tramping over the moors of Devon and Cornwall and up around the Cotswolds . . ."

"Actually, he thinks I could do worse than start at Maidenhead. There are some very fine old coaching inns along the river there, with a history dating back to . . ."

"The Royal Falcon! The penny's dropped at last!" Excitement blazed in Ruth's green eyes. "It's not a bad idea, is it? A photographer doing a feature on the hotel would be allowed to roam literally all over the place."

"Exactly. What Hyde managed to convey was that such a freedom of movement would never be possible for the police unless they had a search warrant; and once that was issued the bird and the money, if they *are* at the hotel, would have flown."

"All the same, it's going to be tricky. I mean, if we just march in and nose around—"

"*We?*"

"Oh yes – *please,* Philip! You'll need an assistant – and think how useful I could be in spying out the land."

She looked so appealing that he couldn't refuse. And she was right; she would be useful, in the task of probing for information.

He threw away the cigarette and smiled indulgently. "All right, Ruth, you can come along. But I must read you the Riot Act first. It could be dangerous."

"Anything for a change after the boredom of daily life in the studio."

Philip started to mention a certain deserted warehouse near St Paul's, but Ruth was not listening. "What exactly are the Inspector's orders?" she asked eagerly.

Philip shrugged his shoulders. "You know Hyde – cautious to the bitter end. The best I could get out of him was a hint that we should keep our eyes and ears wide open and report anything or anyone suspicious that could possibly – and I quote – 'allow the Law to step in and take the matter in hand'."

"In other words, poke our noses all over the place and hop it if things start to get hot?"

Philip laughed. "You seem to have got the message!"

"When do we start – tomorrow?"

"Have a heart, Ruth! These things take time. If I were to appear at the Royal Falcon tomorrow with my camera slung over my shoulder Vanessa Curtis would bolt for the hills! No, Hyde's going to arrange the whole thing in subtle style. Mrs Curtis will get a fearfully impressive letter – a completely genuine letter, mark you – from the Features Editor of one of the big Sunday newspapers. The letter will say that a series in full, colour on the Ancient Inns of Great Britain has already been launched and that the Royal Falcon is something like Number 7 on the list. It'll make it clear to her that she'll receive free publicity from the series, and the hotel will be splashed all over the Sunday Colour Supplement and so on, and will it be all right if the paper sends its team along during the course of the next few days?"

Ruth nodded approvingly. "Pretty good. She can hardly refuse."

"Exactly."

"And when we, the team, turn up on her doorstep . . . ?"

"Again, she can hardly refuse."

Philip was right. Vanessa Curtis did not like it, but having already agreed to allow the hotel to be featured in the newspaper she could scarcely refuse to let them in.

Plucking at the buttons of her dress with nervous fingers, she asked, "How long will it take? I mean, how long will you be here?"

"That's hard to say, Mrs Curtis, but I don't think it'll be more than a day or two."

She seemed to brighten a little at this. Evidently she felt better able to face the strain of having them under her feet if it would soon be over.

Philip introduced Ruth. "This is my secretary and assistant, Miss Sanders. I concentrate on the photographic side of things, of course, and Miss Sanders is responsible for the editorial side – the captions and background story, and so on. She's a stickler for accuracy, so I hope you'll be able to let her have the details of the building – dates of renovation – names of any interesting people who've stayed here . . ." Vanessa Curtis's face clouded and Philip hastened to add, "It's *ancient* history we're interested in, Mrs Curtis. I need hardly remind you that there'll be no mention of recent events. They're unhappy memories for both of us, and I've no wish to be reminded of them any more than you have. No, the only kind of publicity this will give you is good publicity."

She went very white in the face, but made an attempt at a polite reply and rang the bell for Albert, who showed them to their rooms.

The following morning they began their work

Mrs Curtis, in a manner that could only be described as wary, conducted them through the various public rooms of the hotel and related incidents of history connected with each one. Ruth took assiduous notes, as she had often done on previous assignments, while Philip contented himself with a serious and completely professional inspection of potential shots. He took no actual photographs but, as was his normal routine, concentrated on possible camera angles, the quality of natural light or the availability of electric points for the lamps he would use in indoor scenes.

By pre-arrangement there was a telephone call for Philip during the course of the morning. It was the Editor of the Sunday paper who had officially commissioned the series. They talked for five minutes, the conversation exclusively concerned with the work on hand and Philip's next assignment, a smugglers' inn on the Cornish coast. Ruth reported afterwards that Mrs Curtis had excused herself when Philip had been summoned to the telephone. They thought it likely that she had listened in at the hotel switchboard.

They were given a good lunch and over coffee Mrs Curtis joined them, presenting Ruth with a copy of a brochure which gave an account of the hotel's history. Her manner was quite affable, and they took pains to keep it so.

The afternoon was spent in serious indoor photography. They asked permission before setting up each individual shot, and by the evening had so won Mrs Curtis's confidence that she agreed to pose in some of the scenes herself.

"You are the owner, after all," Philip pointed out "And a room without a pretty woman in it is like a garden without flowers?'

"When you turn on that charm of yours," Ruth remarked to Philip afterwards, "no woman alive can resist you."

He looked uncomfortable and dismissed the compliment "It's not my questionable charm that thaws them out, it's the prospect of seeing themselves look glamorous in my pictures which does the trick. You must admit I generally make them look twenty years younger."

"Provided I do the retouching," Ruth rejoined.

"Yes, dear, I just don't know what I'd do without you!" He smiled good-humouredly. "Only this time it's got to be one of Hyde's back-room boys."

"Why?"

"Because I want some prints to show Mrs Curtis tomorrow. If they're flattering it will smooth our path no end. I've got to go up to Town tonight, and your job will be to stay put and keep your eyes peeled. We haven't found out much today and time's getting short."

"I realise that, and I'm worried. What's the plan for tomorrow?"

"Officially, outdoor shots. Actually, I'm praying for rain."

"That sounds like a contradiction. Why?"

"You're dead right. I dare say you've noticed that our hostess hasn't shown us the basement yet. Now there must be wine cellars and food-storage rooms down there. I'd dearly like to get a look at those. And she also seems to want to deny the existence of an attic, but you can see from the courtyard that there's a whole top floor with at least two mansard rooms. Now, why doesn't she want to show us those?"

Philip drove to London that evening and parked his car in clear view of his studio.

Inside, two experts from the Yard's photographic section were awaiting him. He handed them the day's shots, dallied long enough to satisfy himself that the men knew their job, then went through to his flat and let himself out by a back exit. Here he climbed straight into a waiting taxi which took him to his secret meeting with Inspector Hyde. After the successful job of shadowing which the bank thieves had carried out at Windsor no chances were being taken.

Hyde was waiting for him in the back parlour of an unappetising pub in Southwark.

Philip came straight to the point "I'm afraid we haven't found out very much, Inspector."

"I hardly expected you would on the first day, Mr Holt. The vital thing is that you're *inside*. How are you rubbing along with Mrs Curtis?"

"She was pretty shaken when she saw me, but I think she's thawing out gradually. That telephone call from my 'Editor' helped. If I can flatter her with some good photographs things should go a little more smoothly tomorrow."

"What parts of the hotel have you been in?"

Philip told him and added, "She hasn't suggested we go down to the basement yet, nor up to the top floor. I'd very much like to poke around in that attic."

"Tread cautiously, Mr Holt," the Inspector warned.

"We haven't much time. I can only spin this assignment out a day or so longer."

"Quite so. Now then, what about the guests staying at the hotel? Has anyone in particular taken your eye?"

"They all seem ordinary enough. You can see for yourself as soon as my film's developed. They're all on it."

Hyde's eyebrows rose appreciatively. "How did you manage that?"

"Simple. I persuaded Mrs Curtis that one doesn't photograph a dining-room when it's empty. I was able to cover the ground pretty thoroughly during lunch-time. I should think I've managed a good shot of all the guests. I used a telephoto lens, so most of them wouldn't even have realised they were being snapped. And I've got pictures of all the staff, too. You can check them all with your Rogues' Gallery before midnight"

"Excellent."

"All the same, I don't feel there's anyone suspicious there.

If the brain behind the Hamburg bank robbery is at the Royal Falcon he certainly knows how to blend with the landscape."

After a moment's silence Hyde went on, "Assuming that my theory is correct, Mr Holt, assuming that the money is hidden somewhere in the hotel, it doesn't necessarily follow that the master-brain is actually there too. That would be taking a huge risk. But sooner or later, it seems to me, they'll try and move the money. Quite possibly someone will come from outside to pick it up. It might be the man himself, it might be just a middle-man who will lead us to him . . . I don't know. All I can say is, keep your eyes and ears open for all departures and arrivals."

"I'll do that," Philip promised.

For a further hour they discussed all possible aspects of the case, then it was time for the taxi to take Philip back to his flat.

There he found the prints of his day's work waiting for him. The quality of the work done by the Yard's experts almost came up to his own exacting standards. Satisfied, he left copies of the dining-room pictures for Hyde's perusal, then drove back to Maidenhead with the remaining proofs. The scenes in which Mrs

Curtis had figured had come out particularly well, which would undoubtedly be to his advantage.

To Philip's surprise, because it was very late when he reached the Royal Falcon, he found Ruth sitting at the bar with a florid-faced stranger with a bushy moustache. The two appeared to be getting on well and greeted him with a jovial warmth which he had some difficulty in reciprocating. Ruth, her face a trifle flushed, called out to him to join them, but Philip stiffly refused and went up to bed.

Ten minutes later, as he was unknotting his tie and trying to suppress the unreasonable irritation which had suddenly swept over him, there came a tap at his door.

It was Ruth, a mischievous sparkle in her eyes, but with all traces of undue hilarity gone.

"Are you decent?" she called out.

"More or less. Come in." He looked at her curiously. "You certainly seem to have sobered up in a hurry. What was that little scene at the bar in aid of?"

"Don't you like my new boy-friend?" she retorted with a saucy grin.

"Not much. Who is he?"

"His name's Johnny Carstairs. He picked me up this evening after you left—"

"He did what? You ought to be ashamed of yourself!"

"You really are depressingly Victorian at times. It's done my morale a world of good. Two whole days with my nose to the grindstone and no one to take any notice of—"

"Yes, well . . . Is he staying at the hotel, this Carstairs?"

"Yes, he arrived tonight, just after you'd gone. He saw me sitting on my own after dinner and asked me to join him at the bar for a drink. Actually," Ruth went on, her tone becoming deadly serious, "I didn't care for his line at all, nor that dreadful moustache, but it occurred to me that a bar stool, with that long mirror behind the bottles, was an excellent place to watch the proceedings. Far better than sitting in the lounge all evening and peering suspiciously over the top of a newspaper. Through the mirror I kept an eye on the lounge and got quite a good reflection of the main entrance and Mrs Curtis's private office as well."

"I see," said Philip, somewhat mollified by this explanation: "And what were the proceedings? Did anything interesting happen?"

"I don't think so. Mrs Curtis stayed in her office all evening except once, when she brought a pack of bridge cards to a bunch of old girls near the fireplace."

"Did anyone go into her office to see her?"

"Only members of the staff. And my boy-friend."

"Carstairs?" Philip said sharply. "What did he want?"

"He said he wanted to cash a cheque. I took the chance while he was gone to empty the gin out of my glass and substitute water."

"How long was he in the office?"

"About ten or fifteen minutes."

"Rather long, just to cash a cheque."

"Not long enough for me," said Ruth wryly. "The man's a frightful bore. All he can talk about is cars! . . . No offence meant," she added as Philip laughed. "You do have other qualities and other topics. Not our Mr Carstairs, though. I gather it's his job as well as his hobby. He says he's delivering some super-duper French model to a wealthy chap from the north. The man's coming here to pick it up."

"I wonder if it's that two-seater Peugeot 404 I noticed in the courtyard as I drove in," Philip said, "Well now, that makes a very convenient angle for my getting to talk to your Mr Carstairs."

"He's not my Mr Carstairs, I assure you!" Ruth said. "You can have him, and his blessed car. He wants to take me for a ride in it tomorrow. Still, I expect you'll be keeping me busy working, anyway. What do we do if it doesn't rain, Philip?"

He crossed the room and opened the window, staring wistfully at the cloudless sky emblazoned with stars. Rain seemed like a half-forgotten memory.

There was a long silence before he said, "What tomorrow

holds in store, I don't know . . . But get a good night's sleep, Ruth; it could be a hard day."

The following morning dawned bright and clear. After breakfast there was nothing for it but to carry out his stated plan of concentrating on outdoor shots. They managed to waste quite a lot of time photographing the hotel from the banks of the river, then around mid-morning he moved the equipment to the forecourt to obtain close-up shots of the half-timbered façade.

Under the pretext of studying the angles of sunlight and calculating the best time of day for these scenes Philip was able to keep the two mansard windows of the attic under observation. There seemed no signs of life up there, except once when he fancied he caught a glimpse of a pale face behind a partly drawn lace curtain. Mrs Curtis had casually mentioned that the rooms were never occupied and only used for storing trunks and suitcases. His pulse quickening, he ducked behind the black cloth draped over his mounted camera and was eagerly straining for another look when the roar of a car engine disturbed him. A scarlet Peugeot sports model with an open top flashed up the drive, executed a perfect four-wheel drift, and crunched to a standstill outside she main entrance. Johnny Carstairs swung lanky legs over the unopened car door and vaulted out.

"Good morning!" he called to Ruth. "How about coming for that spin I promised you?"

Ruth hesitated, shot Philip a quick glance, then called back, "I'm afraid I can't just now. I'm working."

"Bless my soul, you're taking pictures – and I go and plant my 'cat' in front of the hotel! Still, it would add a spot of colour to the scene, wouldn't it? Shall I leave it there? Or am I in the way? Just say the word and I'll vanish, my dear!"

Ruth began to voice a mild protest, when to her surprise Philip interrupted her. "It's not a bad idea," he said, crossing to the Peugeot "As you say, it does add some life to the picture. Would you have time to manoeuvre it around a bit? I'd like to try several different positions."

"My dear fellow, I'd be delighted," the florid-faced man replied, beaming at them and stroking his moustache. "I've got nothing to do. I'm waiting for this Sheffield steel magnate who's coming down from the north to pick up the 'cat'."

"Oh, it's not yours, then?" Philip asked, eyeing the Peugeot with genuine interest

"No. I wish it was. Absolute dream to handle."

Philip began to ask technical questions, and in a moment they had the bonnet open and were deep in a discussion of the automatic ventilator cut-in and other abstruse matters.

Ruth sighed heavily; this could last for hours. But Philip joined her a moment later and, out of Carstairs's earshot, murmured, "Keep your eyes on the attic, Ruth. Mrs Curtis says it's never occupied, but I could have sworn I saw someone lurking up there just now, the second before your boy-friend turned up."

Then Philip went back to the sports car, while Ruth drifted casually to the far edge of the courtyard and kept careful but unobtrusive watch on the top floor.

By lunch-time nothing untoward had happened. The mansard windows stared blankly at her, people came and left, a large butcher's van delivered carcases of meat, and a vintner's brought crates of wine, while Philip, with Carstairs' aid, took several shots of the hotel exterior, the Peugeot adding a splash of scarlet to the scene.

Shortly before noon the sun disapeared behind growing clouds.

At lunch Ruth and Philip managed to shed the jovial Carstairs and sat at a corner table where their conversation could not be overheard. Mrs Curtis appeared once or twice and seemed acutely nervous.

"There's something up, Ruth," Philip said quietly. "I can feel it in my bones."

"Yes, so can I," Ruth answered tensely. "But what? And where?"

"Hold it! Here comes Madam herself."

Mrs Curtis flitted up to their table. "I hope you won't mind my asking, Mr Holt, but it's about your rooms. Will you be requiring them again tonight?"

"I'm not sure," Philip replied, peering out of the window. "It depends on the weather. The sun's gone in and unfortunately we haven't quite finished outside. We might have to concentrate on indoor work this afternoon and wrap up the final points tomorrow."

"But you said you'd only be here two days."

"Two, or three, Mrs Curtis. I shouldn't want to hand in a slapdash job to my Editor. That would be bad for me, and bad for you and the Royal Falcon."

"But you've already photographed everything there is inside," she wailed.

"Almost everything, I agree," Philip said cheerfully. "But I'd rather like a shot of the forecourt taken from somewhere on the roof, if that can be managed. And I heard that you have a very fine old wine cellar. That ought to go in the feature, don't you think? You knew, picturesque cobwebs, musty vintage, bottles, all that sort of thing."

"It's very dark down there, I fail to see how you'll be able to . . ."

"We'll fix up some lamps. I've brought plenty of extension cable." He gave a chuckle and added, "I promise we won't slip any vintage champagne up our sleeves."

Vanessa Curtis compressed her lips in a tight line, then said stiffly that she would fetch the keys and conduct them to the basement personally.

When she had gone Ruth raised her eyebrows in inquiry.

"She doesn't like it," Philip surmised, "but she doesn't want to excite our suspicion by refusing, I'd say. She'll watch us like a hawk, so it's up to us to grab our chances as and when they come."

"What about the attic?"

"You'll have to see if you can slip up there while I keep her occupied down in the cellar."

"Right"

After coffee Mrs Curtis appeared with a large bunch of keys and led them to the basement.

They traversed long narrow passages and had to step aside as a butcher's assistant in a white coat, a carcase of pig hoisted on his shoulders, passed them and swung the big lever of the metal door to a deep-freeze room. A blast of chilling air met them, and Philip caught a glimpse of poultry and various sections of meat, varying from fillets to complete carcases, hanging on steel hooks.

Then they came to the massive door of the cellar, guarded by heavy padlocks. Mrs Curtis unlocked it and stood aside as they stepped in and gazed at the impressive rows of bottles neatly stacked and labelled in wooden bins. The cellar's curved ceilings and walls were of hewn stone and the floor laid with fine gravel; cobwebs and dust shrouded some of the vintage burgundies and clarets, and Philip inspected some of the labels.

"My word, you must have a fortune invested here," he commented.

"Yes," came the stiff reply. "The Falcon has always had a reputation for fine wine. It's one of the reasons why our wedding receptions and banquets are so popular."

"I can imagine . . . Oh, Ruth – I've forgotten my light-meter. Silly of me! Run up and get it, there's a good girl." Ruth nodded and slipped away, while Philip kept Mrs Curtis in conversation and examined the possibilities of setting up lamps for his photographs. Although she was watching him carefully she could not prevent his inspection of the cellar.

He found nothing definite, yet he sensed that all was not quite as it should be. One of the wooden bins seemed newer than the others, and was almost empty. The wall behind it was not covered with dust. He pretended to drop his tape-measure, and as he went on his knees to pick it up he was able to discern some faint scratches on the floor, extending in a crescent outward from the wall.

Not daring to draw attention to his specific interest in the area around the new bin, he stood up and deliberately concentrated on another part of the cellar. Mrs Curtis was watching him with ill-disguised nervousness.

"Are you sure I'm not keeping you?" he ventured.

She shook her head. She had obviously no intention of leaving him on his own. He began to despair of getting rid of her, when the momentary distraction of Ruth's return caused her to turn her back.

He moved swiftly to the new bin and leant heavily on it. It answered to the pressure, as though on hinges.

Mrs Curtis turned back to him and he stepped casually away as Ruth handed him the light-meter. Her fingers touched his and he felt that a piece of paper was folded underneath them. Her eyes were ablaze with warning.

He adjusted the meter and began to take readings at various parts of the cellar, while Ruth set up the lamps. The paper still lay folded in the palm of his hand and, under the pretence of jotting down some figures in his notebook, he eventually managed to open out the piece of paper and read what Ruth had written.

Before Lunch there were TWO butchers' men in white BRINGING MEAT IN. Now there are THREE men in white TAKING MEAT OUT. Why? (The attic's empty, but someone WAS there – I could smell tobacco smoke.)

Philip's heart missed a beat. In a flash he saw they might be getting away with it. He had to stop them!

"You've brought the wrong light-meter," he said, blundering past Ruth and the startled Mrs Curtis. "I'll have to fetch it myself!"

He slammed the door of the cellar behind him and tore down the passage. As he passed the cold-storage room he almost ran full tilt into a man in a white helmet and overall with a large carcase on his shoulder. The man was leaving the cool-room, not entering it. Ruth's query flashed through his brain. *Why?* It was normal to be delivering meat, but not to be taking it away again.

He stood still for a second, his pulse racing, as the tall figure in white, its back somehow faintly familiar, walked steadily away up the narrow passage. Philip made a split-second decision.

He cleared his throat and called out to the retreating figure, "Wait a moment! Mrs Curtis wants to keep that piece of meat. You can bring it back."

The man continued walking, with only a slight increase of pace.

"Do you hear? Bring that carcase back!" Philip yelled.

The man in white broke into a stumbling run. He was hindered by the heavy weight on his shoulder and in a flash Philip was pounding up behind him. Somewhere in the rear he heard a feminine scream. Philip was scarcely three yards away when the man whirled round, whipped the steel hook from the meat, and hurled the carcase at his pursuer.

Philip swerved in the nick of time, and then let out a gasp. In the action of hurling the carcase the man's white helmet had fallen to the floor.

It was Douglas Talbot who stood before him, his face a mask of fury, the gleaming meat-hook in his hand.

Talbot lunged and swung viciously with the hook as Philip sprang backward. Talbot regained his balance and the hook flashed within inches of Philip's face and buried itself deep in a crate of vegetables. Philip hoisted up the crate, prepared to hurl it at his opponent, but the sight of the gun shocked him to a standstill.

"This is going to be a pleasure, Mr Holt!"

"Don't be a fool, Talbot! You don't stand a chance, you'll never get away with it!"

"Think again, Holt, think again. I've got away with it so far, and they can't pin anything on me if I don't exist. Everyone thinks I'm dead. They can't pin a murder on a dead man, you know."

The gun was levelled at Philip's chest. The finger on the trigger tightened white, and then the narrow corridor reeled to the sound of a deafening report . . .

Momentarily, Douglas Talbot's eyes registered bewilderment, rage, and pain, and then he crumpled slowly to the floor.

Philip stared beyond the sprawled body and saw Johnny. Carstairs with a revolver drooping casually in his fist. "Sorry I didn't make it a few moments earlier, Mr Holt," he was saying: "I was taking care of those fellows out there; had to stop them driving off with some rather valuable meat carcases. Now then, where's your girl-friend? I wouldn't want anything to happen to her."

"Ruth!" Philip roared, racing down the passage to the wine cellar. Oblivious of possible danger he flung open the door and burst in.

A weeping Vanessa Curtis was sitting on the floor in a pool of champagne, a broken bottle beside her, and Ruth standing over her in command.

"Are you all right, Ruth!" Philip shouted anxiously. "What happened?"

"Yes, I'm all right," Ruth replied cheerfully. "Mrs Curtis got a little out of hand, so I just borrowed the nearest weapon." She picked up the remains of the broken bottle. "What a shocking waste of bubbly! I really should have chosen something cheaper."

Chapter Sixteen

A few evenings later Inspector Hyde, Ruth, and Philip sat at a table in one of London's newest restaurants.

"Inspector," Philip was saying with ill-concealed impatience, "this is a charming place and the food is excellent. But I don't quite see what we've done to deserve all this . . ."

"You're far too modest, Mr Holt," Hyde chided good-humouredly. "Both of you. I doubt if we'd ever have solved this case without your invaluable assistance. I wanted to thank you for your help, that's all. There's a pretty firm law that forbids a police officer to accept presents, but there's no law preventing him from giving them. Hence this little dinner party."

"And very delightful it is, too," Ruth interjected. "Don't pay any attention to him, Inspector – concentrate all your charm on me!"

"With pleasure, Miss Sanders. Where shall I begin? By telling you how radiantly beautiful you look tonight?"

"You've already told me that once this evening, but no girl ever gets tired of hearing compliments. Now tell me how clever and useful I was in solving the case!"

"Clever and useful are exactly the words I was going to use. The way you used your head so coolly when Fletcher and his thugs abducted you to that warehouse . . ."

"Have you been able to trace it?" Philip asked.

"Yes. We found a lot of pleasant surprises there. Old lags we were anxious to talk to, some stolen property, a fine assortment of burglary tools, and so on. And I also have to thank you for the way you handled the assignment in Harris's shop, Miss Sanders. Then there's your work on the photographic job at the hotel."

"Flattery will get you everywhere, Inspector!" said Ruth, beaming. She glanced at Philip. "It does a working girl good to know she's appreciated now and then."

Philip shook his head in mock despair. "There'll be no holding her now, Inspector!"

Hyde smiled. "You did rather well yourself, Mr Holt. It was your obstinacy over the key, and what you found out from Andy Wilson that helped me to get on the right track – not to speak of your courage in tackling Fletcher when he went for you with a knife, and in going out alone to Blackgate Common to meet Mrs Seldon. And, of course, it was you who opened our eyes to the significance of the word 'Venice'."

"That's very nice to hear, Inspector. But there are still a lot of gaps to be filled in before I really follow the sequence of events."

Hyde nodded and poured his guests more wine. "That I can well imagine. Where would you like me to begin?"

"Well . . . Talbot, for one thing. It never occurred to me that he wasn't dead."

"No, that's what he wanted us to think. In fact, he devoted his energy to concocting a series of lies and deceptions all along."

The Inspector automatically felt for his pipe and tobacco pouch, then remembered he had decided it would be unfitting in such surroundings. Happily he caught the eye of a waiter and was able to order a cigar. Then he sat back in his chair and began to explain.

"Talbot started by forging your brother's suicide note. There's little doubt that he was the murderer too, but for the moment I'm concerned the steps he took to throw dust in our eyes. After the suicide note he turned his attention to you, Mr Holt. I think he must have found out that you were in financial straits, and that by Rex's death you'd inherit quite a lot of money, so you were the perfect 'patsy', as our American friends say. First he switched the photographs in your showcase. Then, after Quayle was killed by Fletcher, Talbot did his level best to throw suspicion on you by linking your name with Dr Linderhof."

"And how does Linderhof fit into the picture?"

"He's as innocent as a new-born lamb. Talbot took advantage of the fact that the doctor happened to come from Hamburg, in order to give the story a sinister twist. And, of course, the writing on the fly-leaf of the second Belloc book was Talbot's expert forgery too. He was able to do that with the aid of Linderhof's letters arranging his hotel booking. Then Talbot made up the package very cleverly so that it looked as though the book had been posted in Germany. The purpose of that book was simply to lure you out to Blackgate Common, because your interference was becoming a thorn in his flesh. Fletcher had been hired to lurk in the back of Clare Seldon's car and kill you, and that was where Talbot made his first blunder – in underestimating the fury of a woman scorned."

"A woman scorned? You mean Vanessa Curtis?" Philip ventured.

"Quite so. She was the discarded mistress; Clare Seldon was her more glamorous successor. Apparently Mrs Curtis overheard Talbot's plans and realised what a priceless opportunity she had of getting rid of her rival. She contacted Fletcher and offered him a higher price to switch targets. She had no qualms about getting rid of Clare Seldon, but apparently she did have second thoughts about having *your* murder on her conscience as well, so she made that anonymous telephone call to us, warning us you were in danger."

"It's about the only streak of decency she's shown in the whole sordid affair," Ruth put in. "After that she seems to have reverted to type pretty quickly – hiding the German money and harbouring Talbot in the attic."

"Quite so. It's pathetic, but I believe she treasured the notion of winning Talbot back, once her rival was out of the way. Talbot will have made capital out of this – the man was utterly unscrupulous in every way."

"I suppose he persuaded her to build that secret vault behind the wine cellar which I nearly found?" Philip suggested.

"Yes. The money was stored there. Nice and convenient for the time when they arrived in a butcher's van and concealed the money in those meat carcases. It was a clever plan. Who would have dreamed of questioning such an everyday thing as meat being delivered to a hotel? If it hadn't been for the sharp eyes of Miss Sanders they might well have got away with it."

"Surely your chap Carstairs, or whatever his real name is, was in on it too?" Philip said.

"No, as a matter of fact he didn't realise until the very last moment what was going on. You see, I didn't plant him there for the purpose of investigating, but mainly to keep a guardian eye on you two."

"That was thoughtful of you, I must say," Philip said gratefully. "I really thought my last hour had come when Talbot pulled that gun on me. Tell me, Inspector, what made you suspect that Talbot's 'death' in that ditch near the hotel was a fake?"

As if enjoying their obvious impatience Hyde broke off the conversation to ply them with invitations to a liqueur or brandy. Philip refused, but Ruth asked if she might have a Benedictine. When it arrived, along with the Inspector's brandy, he continued.

"Ah yes, the body in the ditch which was supposed to be Talbot's . . . Well, it was the manner of killing which first made me suspicious. All the evidence pointed to it being the work of Cliff Fletcher, but it didn't seem to be a typical Fletcher killing. As you know, he nearly always used a knife. The body we found had been mutilated by some massive instrument – my inquiries at the moment seem to suggest that Talbot used a meat-chopper from his own kitchen. At any rate, it was difficult to identify the victim because the face had been so hideously disfigured. Mrs Curtis fainted when she saw the body. I thought I was going to be ill myself, it was so ghastly."

The Inspector tapped off the ash from his cigar and went on thoughtfully. "It occurred to me that if Fletcher had killed Talbot, as they wanted us to think, he'd have taken the precaution of running through the dead man's pockets in case there was anything incriminating there. In fact, we found a diary with the heavy clue of an appointment with Fletcher. That clue was too heavy; I didn't swallow it And then when I heard a local farmhand of about Talbot's build was missing I put two and two together. Talbot had found out where the Hamburg bank money was hidden and was at large. No doubt he intended hopping out of the country just as soon as he'd smuggled the money from its hiding-place in the hotel. I was convinced there was only one place where he would be able to get help and hide anything as bulky as thousands of German marks – in the hotel owned by his erstwhile mistress."

"Then was it Talbot who left the case full of marks at Victoria Station?" Ruth asked.

"No, that was Luther Harris all right. I believe he got worried after you'd shown him the dance ticket. You see, first Rex was shot, and then they tried to kill Andy Wilson. And when Harris saw his name on the ticket I dare say he wondered whether he was earmarked to be the third. So he decided to hand in the suitcase and try to place suspicion on his two army friends, hoping no one would bother with him after that."

Ruth interrupted. "One thing I don't quite get: who tried to run Vanessa Curtis over that morning in Windsor, and why?"

"That was Talbot again. If he overheard her talking to Mr Holt on the phone he'd have realised that Mr Holt intended to question her about her visit to Rex's room. Maybe he tried to kill her, or maybe he only wanted to scare her into silence, but at any rate the effect was the same."

Hyde's cigar had gone out, and they all pondered for a while in silence while he relit it.

Eventually Philip said, "It was Talbot, Quayle, and Fletcher at the top, then – first bringing off a spectacular robbery and then squabbling over the share-out . . . with Luther Harris as a sort of go-between . . . and Rex and Andy playing the Babes in the Wood. And no single person trusting any other further than he could throw him."

"Plus the two women, Mr Holt. One fluffy little one, who isn't quite so fluffy as she seems; and one arrogant beauty who paid the price of her arrogance – Clare Seldon."

Philip made a grimace of distaste. "I think I'll accept that offer of a brandy, Inspector, just to get the taste of that grimy little band out of my mouth."

Hyde nodded and signalled to the head waiter, but his order was interrupted by the arrival of an eager young commis trailing a telephone in his hand.

"A call for you, sir."

Hyde sighed as the young waiter plugged the cord into the tableside socket. "Excuse me, won't you?" he said to his guests. "Hyde speaking. . . Oh, yes, sir." Imperceptibly he sat a trifle more upright in his chair. "Very well, sir, I'll be right along . . . About twenty minutes, sir. . . ." He replaced the receiver and stood up. "I'm most dreadfully sorry, but you'll have to excuse me. That was the Assistant Commissioner, and he wants to talk about a new case that's just come up. I can't get out of it, I'm afraid."

"Oh, Inspector, how mean of him!" Ruth exclaimed. "I haven't enjoyed an evening out so much in ages. Would you like us to come along and meet your Chief?"

Hyde smiled. "That would be very nice for him, of course, but I'm afraid it wouldn't be very . . . er. . . . orthodox."

"Well, not to worry – you know where to find us if ever you need a slight touch of the unorthodox in the future, Inspector," Ruth rejoined.

Hyde looked at her quizzically. "Do -you really mean that, Miss Sanders?"

"You bet your life I do! It's pretty dull working in a photographic studio, you know."

Philip made some comment which was cut off by the Inspector's thanks. "I might be very glad of the offer, unofficially, one day. How about you, sir?"

Philip smiled ruefully, first at Hyde, then at Ruth. "You've observed the set-up for yourself, Inspector; when 'just a very efficient secretary' chooses to whistle, then the boss has to follow suit."

In silence they watched the Inspector hurry out of the restaurant. Ruth sipped her Benedictine and then chattered about the case until she gradually became aware that her partner was paying scant attention. There was the hint of a frown knitting his brows and she knew him well enough to realise that he was debating some serious issue.

"Is there something worrying you, Philip?' she asked sympathetically.

"Oh . . . nothing – nothing important."

"I know you better than that. Come on, out with it."

"Well, it's just that I . . . well, I can't quite make up my mind about something."

"Is it important?"

"Yes, it is rather."

"Tell me."

"You'll probably be mad at me."

Ruth's heart seemed to miss several beats and she tightened her grip on her glass. "No, I won't be mad at you," she said gently.

"Well – it's that Peugeot we saw at Maidenhead. You know the one, Carstairs was driving it. Quite frankly, I'm sold on it, hook, line, and sinker! I'd been thinking of turning in the Lancia for a Mustang, but since I've seen this French job . . . well, quite frankly, I just can't decide. It's maddening."

Colour came back into Ruth's face and she managed a shaky little laugh.

"It must be an agonising decision to have to make," she agreed. "You have my fullest sympathy."

Lightning Source UK Ltd.
Milton Keynes UK
UKOW03f2338150914

238636UK00002B/345/P